Love Notes

MICHELLE WINDSOR

Michelle Windsor asserts the right to be identified as the author of this work. All rights reserved. No part of this book may be reproduced, scanned, distributed, or sold in any printed or electronic form without direct, written permission from the author. Please do not participate in piracy of copyrighted materials in violation of the author's rights.

While this story was inspired by actual events and places, this is a work of fiction. All names, characters, places and incidents are either the product of the author's imagination or are used fictionally, and any resemblance to actual persons, living or dead, businesses, companies, events or locales is entirely coincidental.

First published April 2018
Copyright © Michelle Windsor 2018
Published by
Windsor House Publishing

All lyrics in this book were written, contributed and Copyrighted © by Tyler Legare 2018
You can find all songs mentioned in the book on Spotify.
Cover design by Amanda Walker Design Services
Developmental and copy editing provided by Kendra Gaither at Kendra's Editing and Book Services
Formatting by Christina Butrum

*To the gang at Kritter's:
Thanks for some of my very best memories.
And to my son, Tyler:
Thank you for the music, for your words, and for
filling my heart with more love than I
could have ever imagined.*

CHAPTER ONE

I look in the mirror one more time and stick my tongue out at my own reflection as I pull my hair into a ponytail. This is as good as it's going to get today. It's over ninety degrees out, and keeping my hair pulled back is the only way I'm going to be able to manage the long, wavy locks as I tend bar. I brush some pink gloss over my lips and leave the bathroom, shutting the light off as I go.

Ten minutes later, I steer my car into the parking lot across the street from the pub where I work. It's just after three, but even though my shift doesn't start until four, it's Friday and it's hot. As the clock strikes five, the bar will fill up quickly, so it's better to arrive a bit early and make sure everything is stocked so we aren't running around like chickens with our heads cut off later tonight.

I climb out of the car, make my way through the parking lot, and cross the quiet street. I can see the dim lights on through the gold and blue 'Hook's Landing' lettering on the large, plate glass window, but otherwise, it looks quiet inside.

"Working tonight, are ya, Sydney?"

"Yep." I shield my eyes from the sun with a raised hand and

stop to talk to one of our town's finest, Sargent Sheldon. "Hot enough out here for you?"

"Oh, yeah, but keeps the riff-raff off the streets, so I'm not complaining."

"Sure, except they'll all be hanging out here in another couple of hours." I laugh and point to the door, indicating I need to get going. "See ya later maybe?"

"Nope. Going home to watch the game and then hitting the hay." He tips his hat and smiles. "You have a good night, though."

"Yep. See ya later, Sarge." I pull the door open, step inside, and sigh in relief as cool air washes over me.

"Syd, you're early!" My best friend Kelly is standing behind the bar, loading fresh bottles of Bud into one of the coolers.

"Hey, Kell Bell! Yeah, figured I'd help get things ready for tonight. Think we'll be busy?" I walk straight to the end of the bar and scoot under the cut-through so I can be on the same side as her.

"Does a bear shit in the woods? You look cute."

A quick glance down at my cut-off denim shorts and black tank top has me wondering what the hell she sees that I don't. I look back at her. "I do?"

"You'd look even cuter if you had cowboy boots on instead of those damn chucks."

"I like my sneakers. Do you know how freaking hot cowboy boots would be today? Are you nuts?"

"You'd get better tips with the boots on, just saying."

I look over her outfit, noticing she's also wearing denim cut-offs, but has on a cute, sleeveless, red and white gingham top, the bottom tied in a knot, revealing her toned midriff. Then, yep, her red cowboy boots finish her ensemble.

"You look hot, and we split our tips anyway. What difference does it make?" I lean over and grab a case of Miller Lite off the floor, throw it on the bar, and start loading them into one of the other coolers.

"The difference is that if you spiced up your look just a little bit, we'd make even more." Kelly huffs and continues to slam bottles into the cooler.

"Are you girls arguing again?"

We both turn our heads as Kelly's mom, who is also the owner of the bar, walks out of the kitchen.

"No," we both reply in unison and break out giggling.

"Uh-huh." Shaking her head, she grabs a glass off the back of the bar and pours herself a Coke from the gun. "Syd, can you move the two tables over in front of the left window into the back room? I've got some new entertainment coming in to play tonight, and he should be here anytime to set up."

"Sure, Shannon. Who's playing?" I finish loading the case of Miller Lite I was working on and throw the empty box on the stack behind Kell.

"Justin Jeffries. He does an acoustic guitar thing and sings. Have you heard of him?"

I look over at Kelly to see if she has before, and we both shake our heads no.

"Is he local?" I squat under the cut-through and walk to the front of the bar to begin moving the chairs away from the tables I need to move.

"Next town over, over on County Road. His parents have the big cattle farm."

"Oh, yeah, I know that farm. I don't know the family, though."

"Well, he'll be here soon, so guess you will now." I watch Shannon go back into the kitchen, and then I lift one of the tables and carry it through the bar and out the door to the back room. I plop it down inside the door and do the same with the second table. When I turn to walk out of the back room, Kelly runs in and waves her hands in the air, hopping in place.

"Oh my God!" Her cheeks are flushed pink, and a crazy smile is plastered on her face.

"Jesus, Kell, what's up?"

"Justin Jeffries is what's up. He just walked in, and Lord, that man is fine." I watch as she fans herself again and blows out a long breath.

"You gonna make it?" Sarcasm drips from my voice but, come on; her reaction seems a bit dramatic. I mean, how hot can the guy be?

She immediately stops jumping and looks at me seriously. "You don't believe me?" Extending her arm, she points to the door. "Go out and see for yourself."

"Fine, I will!" I roll my eyes at her, push the door open, and step back into the bar. Empty. I turn back around and raise my brows. "No one's here."

"What?" She pushes past me into the room and looks around and then at me. "Well, he was just here. I'm sure he'll be back."

"Oh, Kell Bell, what am I going to do with you?" I rub her head playfully and crawl back under the bar. "Have you cut any fruit yet?"

I turn as she follows me under the bar, her eyes still glued to the spot Justin was supposedly adorning only moments before. I snap my fingers in front of her face to break the spell she's under and finally get a response from her. "We need lemons."

"Cool. I'll go grab some out back and get started on those." I walk to the far end of the bar and through the doors that lead to the kitchen and grab a box of lemons out of the fridge. Shannon's there as well, cutting up vegetables and humming quietly to herself as she works. I pull a knife out of the drawer and begin slicing lemons and throw them into a bowl. When the bowl is full, I put the remaining lemons back in the fridge and head back into the bar. I swing through the doors and slam right into Kelly, lemons clattering to the floor in a heap of yellow rinds and juice.

"Jesus Christ, Kelly!" I step back and look down at the mess on the floor. "Watch where you're going!"

"Sorry! Shit, look what I made you do!" We both bend down at the same time to pick up the mess and somehow manage to make things worse by banging our foreheads together, thus causing us both to fall onto our backsides. I throw a hand over the spot smarting on my forehead and can't help the laughter that breaks out as I look over and see Kelly doing the same. Thirty seconds later, we're both laughing so hard, with tears streaming down our faces, that we barely hear the *swoosh* of the front door opening.

"Shush!" Kelly throws a hand over her mouth to stifle her giggles and pops to a standing position. I watch as her eyes grow momentarily wide and her cheeks flush pink before she opens her mouth to speak. "Oh, hi again. You need anything?"

"You okay back there?" His deep voice echoes across the empty bar and trickles down to the floor where I'm still sitting, absentmindedly picking lemons up off the floor.

Kelly shuffles back and forth and gives a nonchalant wave of her hand. "Oh yeah, we're fine. We spilled some lemons. Just picking them up."

"I'd love a glass of ice water if you don't mind. It's hot as Hades out there."

I want to stand up so badly to see the person attached to the voice that already sounds like music to my ears, but I remain frozen in place. Kelly tells him we'll bring some right out and squats back down next to me.

She grins like a cat that just ate the canary, grabs the bowl of lemons out of my hands, and whispers to me, "I told you he'd be back. Go get him some water so you can check him out up close."

"Seriously?" Hissing, I grab the bowl of lemons back out of her hands. "You do it! I'll feel stupid after crawling around on the floor."

Swiping the bowl out of my hands again, this time curling it into the side of her body so I can't take it back, she stands abruptly and looks down at me. "Better make it a whole pitcher, Syd. He's looking pretty hot."

"You bitch!" I mouth silently, then rise quickly, turn, and rush back through the kitchen door to get a pitcher.

HERE'S THE THING ABOUT ME: I'M A PRETTY CONFIDENT GIRL. I can strike up a conversation with just about anyone, whether it be an old friend from school, the local law enforcement, or even the tourists that come from miles away in the fall. That is, as long as I'm not attracted to the person in any way, shape, or form. If I'm attracted to someone, I become a bumbling idiot. Either nothing flows from my mouth, or, even worse, strange words come from some hidden place inside of me, spewing forth at the most unlikely of times. And, please know, this isn't limited to just men, and no, I'm not gay, but a beautiful woman can also be very intimidating and trigger these wonderfully embarrassing traits.

So, it really shouldn't be a surprise that my body reacts the way it does as I make my way to the area Justin is setting up. Pitcher of ice water in one hand, an empty glass in the other, I watch his form as he spins around at the sound of my footsteps. I literally feel myself falter and my steps grow heavy as everything seems to slide into slow motion the minute my eyes lock onto his. Eyes that are as blue and calm as the lake I swim in every summer since I can remember, and possibly just as deep.

A warm smile spreads across his face, and I'm almost certain a look of terror appears on mine. At least, it feels like it, as my eyes open wide and my mouth falls open. My heart rate accelerates to a pace that could rival a run-away train; my skin instantly grows hot and flushes to what I'm sure is a lovely shade of crimson. Beads of sweat break out on my back and neck, and I pray the deodorant I'm wearing holds up to its promise of being the most powerful sweat and odor protection available. *Damn it! I hate when Kelly is right. This guy isn't just good-looking; he's gorgeous.*

Without even realizing it, I've come to a full stop in front of him, stupidly staring while I cling to the pitcher and glass in my hands, my mouth hanging just slightly ajar.

"Is that for me?" Is it possible that his smile just got even brighter? He points toward my waist, and with my gaze following the direction of his finger, I look down at the pitcher in my hand, finally snapping back to life.

"Oh, shit! Sorry!" I set the glass on the table and move to fill it with water, positive he can see my hand trembling as I do. His hand wraps around the glass as soon as I pull the pitcher away. Bringing it to his mouth in one smooth motion, he drinks the clear liquid in four large gulps.

"God, that's good. Nothing tastes better than water on a hot day." Smiling, he holds the glass out in front of me, silently asking for a refill.

I move to refill it, and without thinking, speak. "Even in Hell, people get an occasional sip of water, if only so they can appreciate the full horror of unrequited thirst when it sets in again."

I lift the pitcher away from the glass and look up to find him staring at me, his eyes wide with question. I shrug my shoulders and try to explain. "You said it was hot as Hades. You know, Hell?"

"Yeah, I got the reference." He brings the glass to his mouth again, his eyes staying locked on mine, as he drinks down half the glass before setting it on the table. "You a Stephen King fan?"

"I'm Sydney." I put the pitcher on the table, turn around, and quickly walk away before I can make a bigger fool of myself. "Just let me know if you need more water."

"Thanks." His voice reaches my ears as I scurry away. "I'm Justin, by the way."

I toss a wave over my shoulder and practically throw myself

under the cut-through, finding a snickering Kelly waiting on the other side. "Real smooth, Syd." Shooting her a look to kill, I continue moving until I pass through the doors to the quiet safety of the kitchen.

CHAPTER TWO

Chuckling, I shake my head as I watch Sydney scurry away to the kitchen before I look over, eyebrows raised in question, to the bar. "She okay?"

"Oh, yeah." Kelly waves her hand toward the swinging kitchen door. "She gets nervous and acts a little cuckoo if she thinks someone is cute."

A smile breaks across my face as she slaps her hand across her mouth and scrunches up her eyes. "Shit! Forget I said that. Syd will kill me if she knows I told you that!"

I hold my hands up in surrender and shake my head. "I didn't hear a thing."

"She's not crazy. I promise. My girl is super smart. She just graduated Cum Laude from the university and has been asked back to assist one of her professors in the fall."

"Hey, not judging her one bit." I reach down and pick up the glass she left behind for me and drink some more of the water, silently wondering what the hell I've gotten myself into. My friend John got me the gig here and said the bar is usually hopping on Friday nights, but failed to mention the staff might be slightly bonkers.

All I want is to get through the summer playing as many gigs as possible so I can raise as much money as possible for my move to New York City in the fall. It's the only way I'm going to be able to figure out, once and for all, if I truly can make it as a musician. It certainly isn't going to happen playing in small town USA bars and coffee houses. Not that I don't enjoy playing these places; I love it, actually. There's something special about connecting with a smaller audience, and nothing, absolutely nothing, feels better than when I'm playing my guitar and everything else in the world slips away. If nothing else, both girls working the bar are pretty damn cute.

I finish setting up my gear and, bringing my glass with me, walk over to the bar and take a seat on one of the stools. I really need to get back to the barn to bring the cattle in for the night, but it's so God damn hot out that I'm procrastinating a bit.

"You want something?" the perky brunette, who introduced herself earlier as Kelly, asks as she leans across the bar in front of me. I can't really tell if she's flirting with me, but her cleavage definitely isn't leaving anything to the imagination.

"I'll just have some more water." I point to the glass on the bar. "Still have a couple hours of work in front of me tonight."

She swipes the glass off the counter, dumps the ice and glass in a sink, then grabs a clean one off the shelf. Filling it with fresh ice and water, she comes back and sets it on a coaster in front of me. "Yeah, my mom said you live on the farm over on County Road, the one with all the cows."

I chuckle softly. It's always a bit funny to me that in small towns like this, you're always associated with the house or property you keep or live near, or by the twisted oak that got struck by lightning a few years back, or the old syrup house. "Yeah, that's us. We've got about a hundred head of cattle. I still have to bring them in for the night and feed them."

"You got other folks that work on the farm with you?" She's leaning across the bar again, and I honestly believe she has no idea that the action causes her breasts to almost topple out between the buttons on her shirt. I look down at the ice cubes floating in my water so I don't come off like a complete ass trying to ogle her tits.

"I've got a younger brother, but other than him, it's just me and my parents. We bring extra help in when we hay and breed and what not." My eyes swing to the right as the door at the back of the bar swings open and Sydney walks through. Her eyes lock onto mine and seem to widen in surprise then just as quickly shift away as her cheeks turn a light pink. I keep my focus on her until she comes to a stop beside Kelly.

"Your mom wants to talk to you about the orders for next week." Her voice is soft, and again, I can't help but notice it has a melodic quality to it.

"Okay, cool." She turns back to me and smiles. "See ya tonight, handsome." Winking, she pushes off the bar, turns, and walks back the way Sydney came.

I turn my attention to Sydney, who is fidgeting with a stack of coasters, attempting to square them off, and definitely trying to avoid me. There's something about her that piques my curiosity, and even though I now know I make her nervous, I can't help but try to engage her again. "So, Kelly tells me you just graduated from the university."

Her eyes snap up to mine in surprise like it's the first time she's noticed someone is actually sitting at the bar. She just stares at me for a minute before she finally responds. "Oh, yeah. Last week."

"Congrats. That's pretty cool." I take a sip of my water as I realize she's actually making me feel nervous with her intensity.

She shrugs. "Yeah."

I laugh out loud, my nerves kicking in. "You don't say much, do you?"

She shrugs again, and I have to bite back the smile I'm sure will make her even more uncomfortable. "I do when I have something to say."

"Fair enough." I set my glass on the bar top and stand. "I guess I'll take that as my queue to leave then."

A small frown pulls her pouty lower lip down, and her brow creases as a new look sweeps across her face. "I'm sorry. That's not what I meant. I wasn't trying to be rude."

"It's all good." I smile warmly to let her know I'm not offended. "As much as I'd like to stay here and engage in some more in-depth conversation with you, I've got to go back to work for a few hours."

"Oh, okay." I watch as she reaches up and swipes a long blonde tendril that's escaped from her ponytail back behind her ear. "Guess we'll see you later then."

"Looking forward to it." Before I say anything else to make her feel worse, I give her a quick nod and walk to the exit, back out into the sweltering heat.

FOUR HOURS LATER, I WALK BACK INTO HOOK'S LANDING AND find myself in a completely different world from earlier. The bar is lined two deep with folks either drinking or waiting for another, and every table in the place is full. The jukebox is pumping, and the two girls behind the bar have huge smiles on their faces as they pour, mix, and place drinks down in front of people. They seem to know each and every person on a first name basis. I make a detour over to my equipment, giving it a quick check to ensure everything is like I left it, set my guitar down, and head over to the bar. I plant myself on a stool in the far corner that someone is miraculously vacating just as I approach.

I catch Sydney's eye, and instead of the timid girl I saw earlier, a wide smile breaks across her face. "Hey, you! You want something?" She arches an eyebrow and lifts an empty glass in question. "More ice water?"

"Whiskey, neat. But, yeah, I'll take a water back, too, please." I try really hard to suppress a grin, in an attempt to appear cool, but fail miserably when she playfully responds.

"Oooh, we got a whiskey man on our hands, Kell." She grabs a rocks glass off the shelf, turning to look at me, a glint of mischief in her eyes, as Kelly hands a bottle of Jameson to her. "You know what they say about guys who drink whiskey, don't ya, Kell?"

"They're Irish?" Kelly laughs as she responds.

"Yeah, that works, I guess." She looks up at me with a shy smile as she tips the bottle and pours at least three fingers into the rocks glass. Then, she pulls a shot glass from under the bar and fills it as well. Using her fingers, she slides the glass toward me, picks up the shot glass and looks right at me. "Winston Churchill said that whiskey is the drink that enables man to magnify his joy." She brings the shot glass to her mouth, smiles, and then downs it in one swallow. "What do you say about that?"

My mouth falls open for just the briefest of moments before a grin breaks across my face, my head shaking in disbelief. "Well, you're certainly making things more enjoyable."

"Oh, yeah, she's just the life of the party." I watch as Kelly comes over and grabs the shot glass out of Sydney's hand. "Especially when she has a few shots in her." She takes the bottle of Jameson out of the other. "No shots on this side of the bar."

At least, that helps to explain the personality shift from this afternoon. I can't help but wonder just how crazy these two girls are as I watch Sydney puff her bottom lip out in a pout before laughing. "Yes, Boss."

She turns, grabs a glass, and fills it with ice and water before setting it in front of me. "Your water back."

"Thanks." I stand and reach for my wallet. "What do I owe you?"

She shakes her head and, looking up under her long lashes, treats me to the shy smile I'm more used to. "Talent always gets the first round on the house."

I sit back on the stool and raise my glass. "Thanks, appreciate it."

"Sure. Let us know if you need anything."

Before I can respond, she glides down the bar and starts a conversation with another couple waiting for drinks. I sip my whiskey and, using the mirror over the bar, try to discreetly watch how she interacts with the different people at the bar. It doesn't seem to matter if the person is dressed nicely, the corner bum, young, or old; she has a way of making everyone feel welcome and special. Every single person she serves leaves the bar smiling.

"She's single, ya know." Kelly leans over the bar in front of me.

"Who?" I'm trying to play it cool, but I guess maybe I wasn't as stealthy as I thought using the mirror.

"You know who." She rolls her eyes. "Don't play coy with me. I see you watching her."

"Nah, it's not like that." I take a sip of my whiskey, trying to improve my 'I don't give a shit' ruse. "I was just trying to figure out how she went from barely able to talk to me this afternoon to doing a shot with me."

"She's not a girl you take at face value." She leans over so she's a little closer to me and lowers her voice. "Plus, she did two shots before you came in to calm her nerves."

"So, you're saying I make her nervous?" I cock my eyebrow.

She puts her hand on her hip and shakes her head. "Did you hear anything I said to you earlier? Are you as dumb as you are good looking?"

"Ouch." I chuckle. "I'm not sure which one of you is feistier."

"The girl never does shots. Never." She turns and looks at her friend, who's at the other end of the bar, and then back at me. "I'm sure she has to be feeling pretty darn good after that third one." Her brows crease slightly, and her lips turn down in a frown.

"What did I do?" I raise my hands defensively. "I'm just here to play some music and asked for a drink."

"Uh-huh." She crosses her arms and continues to stare at me. "I'm keeping my eye on you."

"Seriously, you've got nothing to worry about with me. I'm leaving in the fall. Chasing girls is the last thing on my mind."

"Uh-huh." She nods her head a final time, her eyes definitely giving me a look that means business. She glances to the entrance as the door opens, and a broad smile erupts across her face. "Adam!" I seem to be forgotten and thankfully dismissed, as she turns away to greet the man who just entered.

I watch her walk to the end of the bar, duck under the walk-through, and then pop back up and throw her arms around a police officer. "Hey, babe!"

He blushes and kisses her softly on the top of her head, clearly smitten with her, before gently pulling her arms down and taking a step back. "You know I can't do that in uniform, Kelly."

"Oh, Adam, no one here cares." She takes a step toward him again, but he puts a hand out to stop any forward progress, a smile on his face as she stomps her boot on the floor. "You're such a goody two shoes!"

"I'm a cop, Kell. It kind of goes with the territory." He laughs at her little tantrum before bending over and kissing the top of her head again. I'm not sure if it's because he's almost a full foot taller than her and it's easier than bending lower for her mouth, or if it just feels less like breaking the rules. "I was just doing door checks and thought I'd grab a soda and say hi."

I turn my attention away from the couple and catch Sydney looking at me, her hazel eyes locking onto mine just long enough to cause her cheeks to flush before she quickly twists her gaze away and focuses on some task further down the bar. I shake my head, thinking she's like a mouse that's just been cornered by an alley cat. I glance up at the clock to see it's ten 'til nine and figure I might as well get started with my first set.

CHAPTER THREE

*W*hiskey is the drink that enables man to magnify his joy? Ugh. What the hell is wrong with me? I shake my head in disgust for being such a dork. Why do I say these things? I slink down the bar to help one of our regulars, all while hoping Justin doesn't think I'm totally crazy. After making a couple gin and tonics, I sneak a glance back in his direction to make sure he hasn't left the building and see him and Kelly chatting. I'm sure she's probably trying to convince him I'm not completely bonkers, but really, why do I even care? I see and talk to at least a hundred men a day. Granted, none of them have eyes I want to drown in or look like Justin, but that's beside the point. I need to get a grip.

I take a deep breath, straighten my shoulders, and decide then and there to get over myself; or better yet, get over the guy sitting at the end of the bar. I mean, after all, he's just a man, right?

"Hey, how's everyone doing tonight?" I whip my head around at the sound of his voice coming over the speakers and meet his eyes. "Think we can get the jukebox turned off for a bit?" He's talking to me, and I nod my head slowly in response. I reach under the bar and flick the switch to turn off the music. Nodding my head at him again, I feel my cheeks heat when he rewards me with a small smile of thanks. *Yeah, I'm doing a great job getting over myself so far...*

"How about a big thank you to the girls at the bar taking care of everyone tonight?" He claps his hand against the wooden face of the guitar he's holding, encouraging the crowd to follow, which they do, accompanied by a few hoots of appreciation. When they settle down, he shifts and moves a bit closer to the mic. "I'm Justin Jeffries, and I'm going to play for a bit. Let me know if there's anything special you want to hear."

I watch as he strums the guitar and immediately recognize the chords to Pearl Jam's "Just Breathe," one of my most favorite songs, and decide instantly that I'm a fan. But when he opens his mouth and begins to sing, I'm completely and utterly dazed. His voice is beyond anything I've ever heard in this bar before, let alone in my life. A chill travels down my spine and goosebumps break out on my skin as if his fingertips are grazing over me. Every person in the room has stopped talking and is staring at him, listening in awe. And even though I know I'm not alone, I feel like I am. Like I'm looking at him through a telescope, and every single thing is laser-focused and just for my eyes and my ears only. Now, I understand what people say when they refer to having tunnel vision. This must be what it feels like.

His voice is smooth and rich and carries so much emotion with each note as he plays and sings. I literally cannot look away from him. His head is tilted down toward the mic, his eyes are closed as the words flow from him, and I am just mesmerized. Is this what it feels like to be dazed and confused at the same time? Kelly comes up beside me and links her arm through mine as she leans over and whispers in my ear, "Holy shit. He's really good."

I don't want to look away to answer her, so I just nod my head, my mouth open slightly in wonder. I'm wondering what in the hell this guy is doing singing in a bar, in a town with less than five thousand people, hiding away on a farm somewhere, instead of selling out major arenas. He is that good, and it's not just his voice or the way he looks; it's how he plays. How every feeling that a song is supposed to draw from you is now pouring from every person in this room. I've never experienced a situation where a single person holds so many emotions in his control. It's breathtaking to see.

As the song comes to an end, he opens his eyes and looks out across the room, and then smiles as everyone claps and cheers loudly. He seems genuinely surprised by the adoration the crowd is showing, and for once, it's his cheeks that are turning a slight pink as he runs a palm down his face, trying to conceal his bashful response. He raises his hand and then motions for the crowd to sit. "Um, thanks, everyone." He shakes his head as if in disbelief. "You sure know how to stroke a guy's ego."

"I'll stroke more than your ego!" a woman shouts from the back of the room. I glance in that direction and have to chuckle at the table of four girls who seem to be as enamored as I am over this guy as they giggle and point at him.

"Why don't I just sing another song instead?" He strums the guitar a few times, tuning a string, and then begins a soft melody I don't recognize. "This is one I wrote, so be gentle with me."

The crowd goes quiet once more as we all listen and lose ourselves in the music again. The chords of the song are mystical and remind me of wind chimes twinkling in the breeze; light and airy and full of beauty. I want to savor every note, but a customer, who apparently hasn't been hypnotized into a drooling fangirl, approaches the bar and orders a round of drinks for her table. Trance momentarily broken, I tear my gaze away and get back to work.

Nearly four hours later, last call has been served and mostly drank, and only a few folks are left to clear out for the night. Justin took one fifteen-minute break throughout the entirety of the evening and spent it fielding questions from people in the crowd and being fawned over by most of the female clientele. He was a good draw and knew we'd ask him to come back again. How I hadn't heard of him before is a mystery. Kelly and I are clearing off tables and pushing the stragglers out the door while Justin breaks down his gear.

Kelly pokes me in the side and points over to the make-shift stage area. "Does Sheila really think she has a chance with him? I mean, come on. She's wearing more lipstick than Bozo the Clown, and that hairstyle hasn't been in since she was reading *Teen Beat* magazine in high school. And we both know that was quite some time ago."

I roll my eyes and stifle a laugh as I watch Kelly take matters into her own hands and walk their way. "Okay, ladies, it's closing time. Say goodnight to Justin and hit the trail."

The girls groan loudly and stumble toward the exit, promising Justin that they will be seeing him real soon. Justin looks at Kelly and mouths a silent, "thank you", and goes back to packing up. I finish wiping down the tables as Kelly hops back behind the bar. She flips the switch to turn the jukebox back on and throws a five up on the counter. "Make sure you put Patsy on for me."

I grin widely as I snatch the money off the counter and skip over to the music machine. I insert the bill and then punch in the numbers I know by heart for some of our regular songs. As soon as the piano intro for "Crazy" by Patsy Cline starts, Kelly is by my side, pulling me into a waltz as we both belt out the lyrics. We laugh out loud between spins and flailing dip attempts, enjoying the favorite part of our night together. This is the part where we unwind with some of our favorite songs, a drink or two, and gossip about anything exciting that happened that night. As the song comes to an end, we both throw our arms out and croon out the last notes. "And I'm crazy for loving… you!!!!!" Neither one of us has a good voice, but we don't care. We both laugh hysterically when we turn and see the shocked expression on Justin's face.

"It's official, you girls are definitely crazy." A broad grin lights up his face and he chuckles. "I guess my job isn't in any danger, eh?"

Kelly snatches a coaster off the counter and tosses it at him like a frisbee. "Oh, hush! Can't a gal have some fun?"

"You both kinda sounded like a couple of alley cats screeching at the moon on a hot summer night." He ducks again as Kelly throws not one, but the whole stack of coasters at him.

"Well, aren't you just a critic!" She pretends to huff and stomp off, throwing us both a backward glance as she goes, sticking her tongue out for good measure. "I think I'll go load the dishwasher."

I agree that we both totally suck at singing, so instead of throwing anything else, I bend down to pick up the coasters now strewn across half the floor, a smile on my face. As I reach for one to my left, Justin's hand reaches out and snatches it up, as well as some others out of my reach. I look over and realize he's bent down and helping to clean up the mess. "You don't have to do that. I can get them."

He shrugs as he does a kind of duck shuffle to slide over and grabs a few more in the corner. "I don't mind. I think I got off lucky with the coasters." He chuckles and tilts his head toward the direction Kelly went. "She's got just a little bit of a temper, huh?"

"Oh, just a bit." I grab the last coaster I can see and stand, my knees cracking a little as I rise. "But she's all heart, that one. She'd step in traffic for me if I asked her to."

I watch as he straightens and takes a step in my direction before extending his arm to hand me the coasters he's collected. "Here ya go."

I hold my hand out flat as he places them in my palm, his hand face down. Instead of pulling away, he lines his fingertips up with mine and rests them there, the coasters now cocooned within our joined hands. I raise my gaze to his in question but find he's fixated on the little nest he's made. I'm about to ask him what's wrong, but then he speaks. "You have long fingers. I should teach you to play the guitar or the piano. You've got the hands for it."

Then he pulls his hand away and drops it to his side. I can't help but notice as he wipes it on his jeans like his hand is dirty now.

I quirk my eyebrow up in confusion and laugh lightly. "Have you already forgotten about my lovely singing?" I point to myself with both fingers. "No musical skills here at all."

"Singing is all about pitch and breathing. Playing an instrument is about timing and the notes to create a rhythm or a melody. You could learn that."

"If you say so, but I highly doubt it." I look at his gear and then back at him. "Do you want some help carrying any of that out?"

"Don't try to change the subject." He grins mischievously. "Look at you right now."

I look down at myself and then back at him, confusion furrowing my brow. "What?"

"See how you're just absently swaying to this music?" His face lights up when a surprised expression of realization sweeps across my features. "You unconsciously feel the rhythm."

"Well, that's because I love this song," I counter smugly.

He shakes his head and, before I can protest further, takes three large steps toward me. He wraps one of his arms around my waist, while the other grabs onto my hand, and then he's moving, dancing with me. I try to pull away, and in return, he tightens the grip around my waist and holds me closer, his chin resting just above my forehead, my face in the crook of his neck, as he whispers, "Just let yourself feel the rhythm."

I'd love to be able to feel the rhythm. Really, I would. But, right now, all I can feel is the way his hand is pressed flat against my lower back, bringing my chest flush with his hard, lean form. Every time he takes a step or shifts his weight, my hand feels the ripple of muscle across his back and the warmth radiating from him. He continues to turn us, slowly, matching the tempo of the song playing. It's "Linger" by The Cranberries, and the only thought running through my head is that all I want to do right now is linger in this very moment.

On the next turn, the hand against my back gently applies pressure and pulls me even closer, his feet on either side of mine, his knee now between my legs, his head lowering so that his mouth is even with my ear. "See how easy this is?"

I want to turn my head so badly and kiss him, but I've never been the kind of girl who can make a bold move like that. So, instead, I just nod my head and close my eyes, absorbing his warm breath along my neck, and let him sway me in slow circles. When the song comes to an end, I feel him pull his hand off my back, which triggers me to step back from him abruptly. I stare at him, tongue-tied, hoping he'll say something to break the spell I'm under, but instead, he just stares right back at me. A small smile finally pulls at his lips, the same lips I find myself wanting to kiss and am most definitely staring at when the kitchen door swings open and Kelly starts talking.

"Sydney!" I tear my gaze reluctantly away from those lips to look at my friend. "You haven't started cleaning behind the bar yet? What the hell have you been doing?" She looks up, the expression on her face changing to surprise when she realizes she may have just interrupted something.

"It's my fault. Sorry," I hear Justin's deep timbre say from behind me. "I was teaching her about rhythm."

Kelly gives me a *what the fuck* look and starts rambling. "Never mind. It's all good. I'll just bring these empties out back."

I start walking to the cut-through. "I'll come help, Kelly."

She looks at me, her eyes wide and apologetic, clearly sorry she disturbed whatever that moment was Justin and I were having. "No, really! I've got it."

Before I can say anything, Justin interjects, "Okay, ladies, I'm loading up and heading out. Have an early start on the farm tomorrow. I'll see you soon, yeah?"

Kelly frowns quickly in disappointment and then focuses her attention on Justin. "Okay. Thanks so much, Justin. You were great. I'll have my mom call you to set up some more dates if you'd like?"

"Sure, that would be great." We both watch as he carries an amp out the door before we turn back to look at each other.

"What the fuck was that, Syd?" She grabs onto my arm and points to the spot where Justin and I were standing a minute ago.

"Damn if I know." I shrug my shoulders in response and then grab a case of empties off the floor and help her finish cleaning up for the night, my heart still thumping wildly.

CHAPTER FOUR

*I*t's been four days since I played at Hook's Landing, and I can't get Sydney out of my mind. I've been working my ass off out in the fields, prepping over twenty acres to be planted with feed corn for the cattle. I should be exhausted every evening, but instead, my mind races, remembering the way it felt when I held her in my arms. Jesus, it felt good. Too good. Sydney most definitely isn't the love 'em and leave 'em kind of girl, so trying to hook up with her and get her out of my system is not going to be the solution. The problem is, I don't want to be attracted to anyone right now. The last thing I need is a summer romance with heartbreak at the end of it when I leave to go to New York.

But, damn it, even knowing all this, every time I close my eyes, I see her hazel ones, and her soft flushed cheeks, and that puffy bottom lip she chews on whenever she gets nervous. Then, I picture myself chewing on that bottom lip, sweeping my tongue over it, and then finally crashing my mouth against hers. It isn't just how she looks that has me tied up in knots. She pulls these random quotes out of thin air during general conversation that blow me away. Who does that? I've never met any girl as pretty as her, and also as smart as her. She intrigues me. I want to peel back the layers she's hiding behind and find out what else lies underneath.

I haven't heard back from Shannon at the pub about any more gigs, so in a spur of the moment decision, I grab my cell and call, hoping maybe Sydney will answer.

"Hook's." A girl answers the phone, but I have no idea if it's her.

"Sydney?" I figure I have a thirty-three percent chance of it being her so take a shot.

"Nope, it's Kelly. Who's this?" Now, I can tell the difference, because Sydney definitely would be a tad more polite.

"Hey, Kelly. It's Justin." The line is silent for a moment, so I continue, not sure if she knows who I mean. "Justin Jeffries, from the other night."

"Yeah, I know which Justin you meant." I hear glasses clinking in the background and imagine she's pouring a drink or clearing a table. "You looking for Syd? 'Cause she's working at the library today."

"What? Oh, no." No way am I letting her know I was, in fact, calling to see if Sydney was there. "I was actually calling to see if your mom wants to schedule any more gigs. My schedule for the summer fills up pretty quickly."

"Well, just so you know, she works at the library in town during the week until four. Hold on." I hear the phone clunk onto the counter and then Kelly yelling, "Mom, it's for you." I shake my head at her phone etiquette and chuckle lightly.

"Hello, this is Shannon."

"Shannon, hi. It's Justin Jeffries."

"Oh, Justin, hello! I'm so glad you called. I've been meaning to ring you and just haven't had a second."

I chat with Shannon for a few minutes, and we schedule in every Saturday for the next three months. I couldn't be happier. With the Wednesday and Friday night gigs I already have at the

Hollow Tavern, I'll be able to save up a fair amount over the summer. But what's even better, I know exactly where to find Sydney. Also, it's in a place where I might actually be able to have a conversation with her.

I glance at my watch and see it's just after twelve-thirty, which gives me plenty of time for a quick shower and a visit to the library before the afternoon work on the farm. I get up, walk over to my dresser, open a couple drawers to pull out a clean pair of jeans and a t-shirt, and head to the bathroom. Twenty minutes later, I throw on my boots and head out to my truck to make the twenty-minute drive into the next town over.

I slide into a parking space across the street from the library and shut the engine off. Normally, I'd wear a ball cap but feel like it's too informal to wear in a library like I'm going to church, so I leave it sitting on the seat and climb out of the truck, shutting the door behind me. It's strange, but I don't think I've been to a public library since I was in high school and I'm actually a little nervous. I've always felt like you need to belong to a special kind of club to go in and feel welcome. This isn't a big library by any means; it's a small square building with a glass door centered right in the middle of the brick facing. There are windows on either side of the door, each decorated with white wooden flower boxes packed with marigolds.

I stroll up the short walkway, ascend three stairs to a small landing, pull the glass door open, and find myself in an entryway of sorts. There's a metal box with a slot at the top, a sticker attached stating 'book return' along one wall, and a bench on the other. It only takes four steps to walk across the entry before I reach the second door. I pull it open, a bell chiming as I do, and this time when I step through, all I see are shelves and shelves of books. After that, the very first thing I notice is the smell. It reminds me of going into our root cellar; it's the same earthy smell, but instead of being cool and damp, it's warm and inviting.

There are four tables in each corner of the room, each with

beautifully colored Egyptian rugs under them. Each table has a low-lit lamp centered on it, with the green glass shade that I always see in movies, and every table but one is empty. An older gentleman has a few books spread out around him and doesn't even seem to notice that someone else has entered the room. It's so quiet that the saying 'you could hear a pin drop' literally runs through my mind. My eyes scan the rest of the room, and that's when I notice the large counter that is centered directly in the back of the room. Behind that desk is the girl I came to see, sitting on a stool, a book in her hand, glasses perched on her nose, her eyes wide with surprise as they stare at me.

I can't help it. A huge smile erupts across my face, and I lift my hand in a small wave and mouth, 'Hi'. *Jesus Christ, that was smooth.* I watch as she slowly lifts her hand and gives me a small wave back, her stare finally breaking when she seems to blink herself back to reality. She sets the book on top of the desk, removes the glasses, rises from the stool, and moves to walk around the counter as I make my way toward her.

When she comes fully into view, I almost trip over my own two feet. *Holy fuck.* She is like every guy's librarian fantasy come to life. Her hair is actually wrapped up in a bun on the back of her head, and I can see she has a pencil sticking out of it. *Is she using that as a hair clip, or does she keep it there for notes?* She has on a black skirt that's kind of long, not stopping 'til it's a few inches past her knees, but it's tight, showcasing her small waist, where a pink button-down shirt is tucked in. But the kicker, she's got on these black heels that have a strap across the top part of her foot. I think I recall someone calling them Mary Jane's. She's like a Goddamn wet dream, and she's walking right toward me. The girl in front of me now is a completely different version of the girl I met in the bar. I want to strut across the gap separating us, fist that bun in one hand, crash my lips against hers—the very lip she's pulled into her mouth and is chewing nervously as her cheeks flush a light rose color—and press her back against one of the stacks until she feels every inch of me. *What the fuck did I just get myself into?*

I LOOK UP AS I HEAR THE DOOR SWISH OPEN, THE CHIME ALERTING me, and feel the lunch I just finished fifteen minutes ago heave in my stomach. *What the hell is Justin Jeffries doing walking into my library?* I watch, wide-eyed and in shock, as he takes in the library before his gaze finally lands on me. I guess he found what he was looking for because his face lights up with a smile and he waves hello. I put the book I was reading down, slide out of my stool on nervous legs, and make my way over to him. *Oh my God, oh my God, oh my God!*

He almost trips, so I start running in case he falls, but being the girl full of grace that I am, my foot catches on one of the rugs. Now, I feel myself flailing forward, a yelp of surprise filling the quiet room.

"Whoa!" I feel his strong grip wrap around each of my arms, pulling me upright onto my feet and straight into his chest. His very hard, but very soft, t-shirt covered chest that smells like moss and cedar. I inhale deeply as I lift my head to look up at him, my feet still wobbly underneath me, and am reminded again of the lake. Those blue, blue eyes are staring down at me in question, a smile just barely tugging at his lips. "You okay?"

"Yes, thank you." I place both of my hands on his chest to put some space between us, hesitating when I feel the swell of his pecs beneath my palm. His heart is thumping ferociously, and I can't help but wonder if he's just as nervous as I am. With my feet steady again, I take a step back and move my hands to smooth down my skirt. I sweep the back of my hand over my face to brush away some strands of hair that came loose, jumping when I feel his fingers graze over mine as he helps to tuck them back in.

I bite my lip, not sure how to respond, and take another nervous step back before looking at him again. "Did you need something? I've never seen you in here before."

"I need something!" Mr. Arnold huffs out from the back table. "I need you two to quiet down. Can't you see I'm trying to get some work done here?"

I roll my eyes and turn toward the only guest in the library. "So sorry, Mr. Arnold. We'll keep it down." Then, I turn my attention back to Justin. "So?"

"So?" His expression looks confused.

"Can I help you find something?" I whisper, but say it slow, enunciating each word to make sure he understands what I'm asking, and in return, he tilts his head and smiles.

"I think I found what I came in for."

I rear back slightly, not quite sure what he's insinuating. "You mean, me?"

His smile grows even bigger, and he nods, "Yeah, you."

"Oh." I definitely wasn't expecting that. "Why?"

Mr. Arnold grumbles something under his breath, so I turn back toward the counter and motion for Justin to follow. "Let's go to the office so we don't disturb Mr. Arnold anymore."

"Okay, sure." His footsteps sound on the hardwood floor behind me, so I know he's following, but I still flinch when I feel his hand rest flat against the small of my back. He's doing it to be gentlemanly, and probably to make sure I don't trip again, but damn if it isn't one of the sexiest gestures a guy has done for me in a very long time.

When we reach the office, I make sure to leave the door open and then point to the table in the corner of the room. "Do you want to sit?"

"Sure." Before I can take a step, he's moving in front of me and pulling out a chair for me to sit in. *I may die and go to Heaven right now. He's insanely gorgeous, can sing, and has manners.* I sit and shuffle forward as he pushes the chair in, and then watch as he sits, not across from me, but right beside me.

"Kelly told me you work here, so I thought I'd stop by." His words rush out, confirming for me that he's nervous, which actually makes me feel better. At least, I'm not the only one who feels like a herd of horses is galloping in their chest.

"Um, yes, at least for the summer. I'm not exactly sure what I'm going to do after that."

"Kelly said you were offered a position at the university in the fall, though?"

I shake my head and frown. "Well, that Kelly sure is a wealth of information, isn't she? What else did she share with you?"

He laughs and covers my hand with one of his large ones, trying to comfort me I think, his thumb sliding back and forth against my skin. "No, it's not like that. She was being protective of you, telling me you're really smart and just graduated."

"Uh-huh." I suck my lower lip into my mouth and nibble it nervously. God knows what will come out of my mouth at a time like this, so sometimes, chewing my lip is the better option.

"Hey." He reaches up and pulls my lip from my teeth, my eyes darting to his in shock. "You're not going to have anything left if you keep chewing on that."

"Sorry." I peek up at him under my lashes, my lip still tingling from the touch of his fingers pulling it from my mouth. "You make me a little nervous."

He looks down at his hand over mine and squeezes softly before looking back up at me. "I'm a little nervous, too, if it makes you feel any better."

"What? Why?" My voice raises slightly in disbelief, even though I know he's telling the truth; I felt it in his chest earlier.

"Well, look at you." His hand lifts off mine momentarily and sweeps up and down in front of me. "You're beautiful, and smart, and not like any other girl I've ever met before."

I stare at him, dumbfounded. *He thinks I'm beautiful?* I've always thought of myself as a nerdy little bookworm, traveling a thousand different miles through the books I've read and characters I've discovered in them. Pretty, possibly, but no, definitely not beautiful. "I think you're the beautiful one, and your talent is just... I don't even have the words to describe how good you are, and I want to be a writer."

"You want to be a writer?" Curiosity laces his voice.

I know I'm blushing again. I can feel my cheeks heating. I've wanted to be a writer since I read "The Little House on the Prairie" by Laura Ingalls Wilder. I shrug my shoulders and nod. "That's why I'm not sure where I'll be working at the end of the summer. If I can, I'd rather work part-time and write as much as possible."

"Have you written anything yet? I'd love to read something if you have." He seems genuinely interested, and it's nice—really nice. There aren't many guys in a small town like this who have an interest in anything besides hunting and driving their trucks in the mud.

"Nothing I'm ready to show anyone," I say quietly.

"Well, maybe sometime then. When you're ready."

I nod my head and give him a small smile. "Maybe."

"Sydney!" Mr. Arnold is standing on the other side of the counter, crotchety as always. I rise and walk quickly out of the office to see what he needs.

"How can I help you, Mr. Arnold?" I give him my most patient smile.

He glances behind me and then lowers his voice. "You going to be okay if I leave you alone with him? I'm about done for the day."

I smile and realize maybe there are still a few gentlemen left in this world after all. "Thank you, Mr. Arnold. I think I'm safe."

He nods and responds gruffly before stalking toward the exit. "Well, all right then. I'll see you tomorrow."

"Bye, Mr. Arnold. Have a good afternoon." I watch him walk away, smiling, and then grow still as I feel the heat of Justin's body behind mine.

Suddenly, I feel his warm breath against my ear as he whispers, "Are you sure you'll be safe?"

I spin around and find myself only inches from his face. My eyes rake over his features, and I notice he has a small scar above his right eyebrow. I lift my hand and trace it with a single finger, his eyes closing as I do. "How'd you get this scar?"

His eyes open slowly and lock onto mine, a simmering look in them. "I fell out of the loft a few summers ago and banged my head on the ladder on the way down. My dad didn't think I needed stitches so it healed like that. It was like a tiny flap of skin ripped back. He just slapped a band-aid on it and told me I'd be fine."

"It looks like a music note." I move my finger away and take a couple steps back from him. "I should probably get back to work."

He looks around the empty library and scoffs. "It's pretty busy in here."

"I have books that need checking in and cataloging to do." I defend the quiet library and my station in it.

"So, what do I need to do if I want to take something out?" A small grin lifts the corners of his mouth as he looks at me.

"You want to take out a book? You need a library card."

"I was thinking more along the lines of the librarian?" His grin goes a little lopsided as he spits his question out.

"Oh." I finally comprehend what he's asking, and a hot flush runs down my entire body in response. "Oh!"

"Do I need to fill anything out for that? Or, maybe, I could just leave you my number?"

"You want to take me out?" I admit I want nothing more than to spend time with him. He's gorgeous and funny and seems to see something in me that others don't. But I'm still surprised because he's gorgeous and funny and seems to see something in me that others don't.

"Yeah, I'd really like that." He's scuffing his shoe back and forth across the edge of one of the rugs, and it dawns on me that he's waiting for me to answer.

"Yes!" I blurt, putting him out of his misery. "I'd love to do something."

His entire face lights up. "Really? Awesome." He's nodding his head up and down like he's not sure what to ask next, but then he continues. "Okay, so you work here every day?"

"Monday through Thursday. Mrs. James works the weekend hours since I'm generally at the bar."

"Do you want to do something on Friday then? You can come out to the farm, and I'll show you around. I can show you what I do. Or, if that's not good, we can do something fancier like dinner and a movie?"

I smile brightly, loving the idea of going to the farm. "The farm sounds great. I'd love to see what you do."

"Great. It's a date. Should I come pick you up?"

"Oh, no, I can drive out. What time should I come?"

"How about one? I'll be done with most of the big stuff for the day by then."

"One's good." I smile shyly, not sure what to say next, but then he walks over to the counter. He grabs a library card and a pen and starts writing, then hands it to me.

"That's my number. Just call me if anything changes."

I take the card in my hand and laugh when I look down to read it. Under the 'due date' column, he's written Friday, and beside it his name, and then finally, underneath that, his telephone number. When I look back up, he's halfway to the door. "See you Friday."

He turns back and gives me the sexiest grin I've ever seen. "Can't wait." I thank God that no one is in the library because as soon as the door closes, I break into the silliest happy dance ever and then race to my phone to call Kelly.

LOVE NOTES

CHAPTER FIVE

"You are so not wearing those Goddamn sneakers."

I look down at my feet and then back at Kelly. "Why are you always making fun of my sneakers? I love my Converse!"

"No. Just no." She walks over to my closet, digs around on the floor, and then turns around holding up my brown cowboy boots. "These are what you need to wear."

"I'm going to visit him on his farm, not the damn rodeo." I frown and shake my head no.

"It really doesn't matter where you're going. It's about how you look, and right now, you look like you're going shopping at Walmart."

"Ugh!" I stomp my foot. "You're driving me crazy!"

She reaches back in my closet, pulls out a tan, loose-knit sweater, and walks over to me. "Besides, it's supposed to rain later so boots will be better." She holds the sweater out to me. "Here, put this on instead, but put your white tank top on underneath first. The one with the wide straps."

"What's wrong with what I have on?" I look down at the faded denim cut-offs and black t-shirt I'm currently wearing.

"It's boring, that's what." She shakes the sweater at me impatiently. "Just do it. You know I'm right."

I let out a huff of defeat and grab the sweater out of her hand. "Fine. Anything to shut you up at this point." I pull the t-shirt over my head and toss it to the floor as I walk to my dresser to find the tank top Kelly insists I must wear. Locating it, I pull it on and then the sweater.

"And you are not wearing your hair up in that ponytail either. It's coming down."

I glare at her as I adjust the sweater to fall off one shoulder, exposing the strap of the tank. "You get that I'm not going to a fashion show, right? I'm going to a farm. There are cows, and mud, and hay, and shit."

"That doesn't mean you have to look like you work there. You need to stand out."

I put my hands on my waist and jut one hip out. "Stand out against who exactly? The cows? His mother? This is complete overkill."

She shakes her head as she tosses me a pair of socks to put on under my boots. "You'll thank me for this later, trust me."

"Uh-huh, we'll see." I sit on the bed and pull on the socks, then slip my feet into the boots. They really are sweet boots. I got them a few years ago in Nashville when Kell and I visited, but I haven't worn them much since. She lives in hers. I'm about to stand when I feel Kell pull the elastic from my head, freeing my hair, it's length falling halfway down my back. "My God! You are such a bitch!"

"Oh, get over it. Go look in the mirror and see how awesome you look." She shoots the elastic at me in a slingshot fashion, and I have to duck so it doesn't hit me in the face.

I run my fingers through my hair to loosen it up a bit and am surprised when I see my reflection in the mirror. I actually do look pretty cute. The wide holes in the knit of the sweater make it look casual instead of dressy, and the cowboy boots are actually kind of sexy with the shorts. I look over and scowl before sticking my tongue out at her. "You win."

She grins smugly. "I always do." She reaches across my bed and grabs her purse, pulling something out of it. "And, here, take this just in case." A shit-eating grin spreads across her face.

I look down and see the tell-tale square foil package between her fingers and feel my face heat up. "Jesus, Kelly! I'm not going to have sex with him! I barely know him."

"Well, it's always good to be prepared. He's mighty fine looking." She thrusts it toward me. "I sure wouldn't say no if he asked."

I push her hand away and stomp in the opposite direction. "Um, aren't you forgetting about one little thing?"

"What's that?"

"Your fiancé? You know, that big guy that wears a gun?"

She laughs and whips the condom in my direction. "Who do you think told me to give you this?"

My mouth drops open in shock. "Well, aren't you two just special, looking out for me?"

"Hey, I don't want my maid-of-honor all knocked up at my wedding this fall. I need you looking hot for my pictures."

"Yeah, yeah." I wave my hand at her, dismissing the 'sex' topic. "Okay, I guess I better head out. It's quarter 'til one, and I'm supposed to be there at one."

"Go!" Kelly hands me my purse and pushes me out of my bedroom, into the main living area of my small apartment. "I'll lock up."

"Okay, thanks." I grab my keys off the kitchen counter and turn to give her a quick kiss on the cheek before I leave. "Make sure Simba's in here somewhere."

"He's in the bathroom. I saw him curled up on your pile of dirty clothes in there." She grimaces. "Maybe time to do some laundry?"

"Okay, leaving now." I throw my hand up in a wave as I walk

through the door. "Thanks, Kell. Bye!" Before she can make me any later, I pull the door shut behind me. I run down the steps, get into my car, and start it up. Justin lives in the next town over, which is only about seven miles away, but it's a simple two-lane road that gets me there, so I hope I don't get behind some slowpoke since I'm already running late.

I get through both of the street lights in town with green lights and smile, relaxing a bit as I cruise out of town. It only takes about ten minutes before I'm crossing over my town line into his, and that's when my nervousness starts. *Holy crap! I'm really doing this. I'm going to visit him at his farm.* It's not like I haven't dated guys before, and I'm certainly not a virgin, but there's something so unique and different about him. Besides, let's face it, he's definitely the best-looking guy I've laid eyes on, even after attending an Ivy League college where rich, good-looking guys are a dime a dozen.

I think, with Justin, it's so much more than how he looks; it's how he looks at me like he can see all the way inside of me and tell what I'm thinking. The fact that he seems fairly intelligent and can sing isn't hurting things one little bit either. I let out a long, nervous sigh as I turn down the driveway to his farm and grip the steering wheel a little harder, my hands slipping slightly from the sweat coating my palms. As I turn the last corner, I see him leaning against his pickup truck, a tight white t-shirt outlining every groove on his chest, tucked into faded jeans, and yes, he's wearing cowboy boots. He waves and gives me the most beautiful smile. My stomach instantly feels like a thousand birds just took flight. Oh. My. God. The man looks good enough to eat. Why didn't I take that damn condom?

I HEAR A CAR COMING DOWN THE DRIVE BEFORE IT'S WITHIN SIGHT, but knowing it's going to be her, I lean back against the truck, trying to look casual. I've actually been pacing around out here for about fifteen minutes, antsy as hell, waiting for her to show up. When she opens the door and steps out of her car, I inhale a deep breath and realize it was worth every bit of the wait.

Her hair is down. It's the first time I've seen her when it's not up in a ponytail or a bun. While I loved that librarian look she was sporting the other day, this is even better. Her hair is long, longer than I would have thought, and falls in soft waves of gold over her shoulders. And that sweater, showing off one shoulder like she's giving me a tiny peek at what lies underneath, but not too much, so she can keep me guessing.

I run my gaze over her, and holy shit! I definitely appreciated her legs the other night when I saw them in shorts, but seeing them now, in a pair of cowboy boots, I think I've died and gone to Heaven. Every time I see this girl, she shows me another side of her. I remember thinking the other day that she was like an onion with layers to peel, but now, I think she's like a rose. A rose whose petals are slowly starting to open and bloom.

I push off the truck and walk toward her, my big steps quickly closing the distance between us. She's biting her lower lip again, and her hands are clenched into tight little fists, so I know she's nervous. I reach her and we both stop short and smile.

"You look beautiful." I reach out and run my fingers through the ends of her long strands. "I like your hair down."

Her hand reaches up and plays with the strands I was just holding, "Thanks. Kelly made me wear it down."

"Well then, tell her I said thanks. She did good." I reach down and grab her hand in mine, her eyes going wide as I do. She doesn't pull away, so I grip a little firmer and turn toward the barn. "Want to go check out the barn?"

"Sure." She walks beside me, quiet, her damp hand feeling tiny in mine, her pulse hammering against my thumb. I wonder if she can feel mine beating just as hard. I think I jump a little when she speaks. "So, you don't work in the afternoons?"

"Sometimes I do. Depends on the season. This time of year, we're prepping all the fields for planting. We grow most of the corn that we'll feed the cattle over the winter. During the summer, we mostly graze them out in the pasture."

"Do you have to milk them? I mean, do they come in every night?"

"We only have a few heifers. Most of our cattle are cows, but we have a few bulls. So, yeah, we have to bring them in each night to milk those not pregnant. We're a dairy farm, so we produce the milk and it's sent out for cheese, yogurt, butter. Stuff like that."

She stops and so I do, not wanting our hands to become disconnected, then she looks up at me confused. "Sorry, I should probably know this, but what's the difference between a heifer and a cow and a bull? Aren't they all just cows?"

I can't help the small chuckle that escapes at what seems like such a simple thing to any of us on the farm. "Don't laugh at me!" She swats at me playfully, and her cheeks flush a light pink color.

"I'm not. I swear. I think it's cute that you're so damn smart but you don't know something that seems so basic to me."

"Well, I'm not really a farming kind of girl." She shrugs and gives me a lopsided smile.

"Yeah, I kinda noticed that, not that I'm complaining." I pull her hand to start walking again and try to explain the cattle. "A heifer is just a young female cow. They haven't had a baby yet, and until they do, they don't produce milk. They take a couple years to mature enough to have a baby, or a calf, so in general, we sell most of them off. A grown female is called a cow. She can produce milk once she's had a baby, but we need to keep her producing milk, so she needs to keep having calves. This is where the bulls come in, the grown males." I look over at her and raise an eyebrow. "I think you can probably figure that part out on your own."

She nods rapidly and raises her free hand. "I got it. Thanks."

We're in the barn now and move inside where it's darker and cooler. It's quiet because all the cattle, with the exception of a few cows waiting to give birth, are out in the fields. My dad and brother are out planting, and my mom's probably in the main house somewhere or prepping her vegetable garden. "Have you ever been to a dairy farm before?"

She shakes her head and looks around. "Nope, I don't think I have. It's big in here. How come there are only a couple cows in here?" She points to the far corner of the barn where they are.

"Those girls are pretty pregnant right now and could go at any time, so we keep them in here where we can keep an eye on them. It's a lot harder to deal with them if they start birthing in the fields."

"Oh." She pulls my hand and moves in their direction. "Can we go see them?"

"Sure." I let her guide me over to them and then quickly position myself between her and the cow. "You want to make sure you stay up by her head, not anywhere behind her hooves. She's a little nervous right now, and I don't want her kicking you."

"Oh, okay, I didn't realize." She seems embarrassed and moves a few steps away and in front of the cow.

I turn and grab her hand to pull her closer to the cow and then place her hand on the cow's neck. "You can pat her. This is Maisy. She's a good girl, just gets a bit cranky when she's about to pop."

She takes a timid step forward, runs her hand gently down the neck of the cow, and begins crooning to her. "Hey, Maisy. Aren't you a pretty little momma cow." Maisy turns her head back and nudges Sydney's hand with her wet nose, an affirmation, which brings Sydney's head around to mine, a smile beaming from her face. "I think she likes me!"

"I think she does." We spend the next forty minutes walking through the rest of the barn, where I show her how we milk the cows and store it, and where the feed and hay are kept. She seems genuinely interested and asks me a million questions. As we exit the barn, I point to the main house and explain that it's where my parents and brother live, and then point out where we plant the different crops.

"You don't live here with your parents?"

"I live in the old caretaker cottage just on the other side of that knoll. I think they got tired of hearing my guitar all hours of the night, so they kicked me over there a few years ago." I point in the direction of the cottage. "Do you want to see it?"

"Sure, I'd love to."

"You okay to walk? We can drive the truck over if you want?"

She looks up at me and smiles. "I think I can manage to walk that far. I'm not that much of a princess."

"Hey, I was just trying to be a gentleman." I give her a devilish smirk and take off in the direction of the cottage. "So, now that you know everything about me, do I get to ask you a few questions?"

"You can ask." She grins at me mischievously. "But I'm not going to promise that I'll answer."

"Fair enough." I walk a minute, thinking about what to ask her first, and decide to start with the basics. "Okay, let's start with the easy ones. How old are you?"

She laughs out loud and gives my hand a little jerk. "Don't you know that you're never supposed to ask a woman her age?"

"Oh! You're a *woman*. Alrighty then, I'll go with thirty-eight. You've got a few wrinkles coming in around your eyes, and yep, I think I see some age spots as well." I bend over and examine her face. "You actually may be too old for me. Maybe I should just walk you back to your car now?"

"Oh, hush!" She giggles and lets out an exasperated groan. "I'm twenty-three. How old are you?"

"I'm twenty-five, so we're actually pretty close in age." I look over at her and smile. We're cresting the hill now and can see the cottage up ahead.

"Oh!" She reaches up with her hand and stretches it flat. "I think it's starting to rain." She looks up at the sky and flinches when a few drops land directly on her face. She laughs and looks at me, her eyes bright with delight. "Definitely starting to rain."

No sooner are the words out of her mouth, a loud rumble of thunder echoes across the valley, the skies open up, and rain pours down. "Shit! Run!" Gripping her hand more tightly, I run with her across the rest of the field until we're up on the porch of the cottage. I throw the door open and pull her inside where it's dry. We're both drenched and dripping water everywhere on the floor, but one look at each other and we burst out laughing. I'm not even sure why we're laughing, but we can't seem to stop. We finally get to a point where we are just lightly wheezing, and that's when I notice that her soaked shirt is basically transparent.

She must see the shift in my expression because she looks down to where my gaze is locked and then gasps, throwing her hands up to cover her peaked nipples under the wet fabric. "Oh my God!"

"Sorry!" I throw my hand across my eyes. "I didn't mean to look. I mean, I looked down, and then I saw, and I know I should have looked away, and I was going to, but... Oh, shit." I spin around and, uncovering my eyes, walk across my small living room area and into the bathroom. I grab a towel and, looking down at the floor the entire time, walk back to her and hand it to her. "Here, take this. The bathroom is right back there." I point. "I'll get you something dry to wear."

She plucks the towel from my hand and dashes past me into the bathroom, the door shutting quickly behind her. Okay, I know I should feel worse, but damn it, I don't. Seeing her wet and exposed like that made me want to peel that shirt off her and see what one of those wet nipples would feel like between my lips. Fuck, now my dick is getting hard. I need to change my train of thought.

I walk to my bedroom and peel off my own wet shirt and then my jeans. I'm pulling on a dry pair when I hear the bathroom door open behind me. I turn around and just about lose my fucking mind. She's standing there, wrapped in just the towel I gave her, her hair tied in a knot on top of her head, and she's staring right at me.

CHAPTER SIX

Sweet mother of all things holy, including the way Justin looks without his shirt on. I mean, come on! Who looks this good? It's just not fair! I was having a hard enough time being around him with his clothes on, and now that I'm seeing him like this, how am I supposed to even function? My eyes travel down the length of his torso—his perfectly sculpted, lightly bronzed, all the bumps in the right places, torso. He's not bulky at all. He's lean and firm, and oh my God, my fingers are itching to follow the trail of hair that starts at his pecs and travels in a dusty line right down to the opening of his jeans.

"Stop looking at me like that." It comes out low and slightly resembles a growl.

"Like what?" I volley back in defense, trying to avert my eyes. "I just wanted to see if you have a shirt I can borrow."

He walks to the closet, pulls a shirt off a hanger, and stalks slowly in my direction, his eyes traveling the length of my body, making me suddenly aware of how very naked I am under this towel. I step back as he continues to move forward, until I bump up against the wall, stopping me in place. When he's directly in front of me, he finally stops, but leans in, placing the hand not holding the shirt on the wall beside my head, effectively trapping me in place.

I slowly raise my eyes to look into his. His brows are furrowed, his eyes dark, his breath warm as he lets out a long sigh. He's so close I can feel the heat radiating off his body and am surprised steam isn't rising around us. "I really want to kiss you right now, but I'm a little afraid."

My heart stutters in my chest before I can speak. "Afraid of what?"

He leans in even closer and whispers, "I'm afraid I'm never going to want to stop." And then his lips are against mine, and they are so warm and so soft and feel like they were meant to fit mine. The world feels like it's shifting on its axis, and I reach out until my hand wraps around his bicep to try and keep myself from falling. I hear the soft *swish* of fabric as the shirt he was holding falls to the floor. His hand grips the back of my head instead, my hair falling out of its makeshift bun and around my face. His other hand leaves the wall and brushes the hair away to cradle my face, his body shifting to press against mine.

And, yes, his body is just as warm as I thought it would be, my grip loosening on his arm so I can wrap it around his neck. His kisses are light and gentle and in stark contrast to how hard his body feels, making me want so much more. I wrap my other hand around his back and pull myself tighter to him, my leg wrapping around his, my towel raising to an X-rated level. His hand shifts to my leg and grasps onto it as he rocks his pelvis into mine.

My head falls back against the wall as I moan at the ripple of desire that just tripled when his hard length rubbed against my core. I can feel how wet I am and wonder for a brief moment if evidence of that just transferred to his jeans. That thought is quickly washed away when his mouth moves down my neck, first nipping lightly, followed by his tongue soothing away the sting of his little bites.

I can't help myself when my hand slides down his bare back,

into his loose jeans, and latches onto his ass to push his hips back into mine. I grind into him, and the scratch of the denim rubs against my clit, my entire body tightening at the sensation.

"Tell me to stop right now or I'm not going to be able to." His mouth is at my ear, his teeth latching gently onto my lobe as he lets out a tortured breath.

I turn and move my lips so I can capture his mouth with mine and start to pull him closer when the front door suddenly swings open.

"Yo, Justin! You here?" A young man, wearing a wet, yellow rain slicker is standing in the door frame. Luckily, we see him before he sees us, and Justin spins around and stands in front of me, his body effectively blocking me from view. I look down to make sure the towel is still in place and find that, thankfully, it is.

"What the fuck, Jonathan? Knock much?" The flat of my hand is on Justin's back, and I can feel the vibration of his anger through his skin. "Wait outside!"

"Shit!" I hear some stumbling and footsteps and then the door shutting. "Sorry, man! Didn't realize you had company."

Justin bends down, swiping the dropped shirt off the floor, and then rises, spinning back to me. "I'm so sorry. That's my idiot brother." He places the shirt, a blue denim button-up, in my hands. "Let me go see what he wants."

I nod my head, my tongue frozen in place, then slide one naked arm and then the other into the soft shirt as I watch him walk outside. I turn my back to the door and then pull the towel loose so I can button the shirt. It falls to my thighs, covering all the important bits, but my nipples are still being traitorous and poke at the fabric. I secure the last button and turn when I hear the door open and Justin walk back through.

"Looks like Maisy's going to calve today. Jonathan and Dad need me down at the barn." His eyes slide down my body and then back to my face as a smile graces his lips. "You look good in my shirt."

I can't help the roll of my eyes. "Cliché much?"

He shrugs and I watch as he pulls a t-shirt out of a drawer before yanking it over his head and then down over his torso. I want to sigh in disappointment, but I did just make a comment about clichés so bite my tongue.

"Just know what I like when I see it." His lips turn up in a cocky grin. "Will you be okay here for a little bit? There's a dryer in the closet in the bathroom that you can use for your clothes.

"Sure." I clench my fingers around the cuffs of the too-long sleeves covering my hands and shift in my stocking clad feet when he stops in front of me.

"Sorry we got interrupted." He leans in, and his lips brush lightly against mine, warm and dry. "Make yourself at home. I'll be back as soon as I can."

"Okay," I manage to squeak out.

"You're so Goddamn adorable when you blush." His face lights up with a wide grin, and then he's out the door.

SIX LONG HOURS LATER, I WALK OVER THE KNOLL AND BACK TO the cottage. I think it's got to be just after eight, as the sun just set, and shake my head in frustration at making her wait so long. The cottage looks dark so I wonder if she left. I didn't even think to look to see if her car was still in the drive when I left the barn.

I step up onto the porch, slide my muddy boots off, and then open the door. I switch on a lamp, washing the room in a soft glow, and frown as I glance around the room and note it's empty. I pull my shirt over my head and unbuckle my belt then my button and let my jeans slide down my legs before stepping out of them. I'm covered in slime and just want a hot shower. As I walk past the couch, I see a piece of paper with words scribbled on it. At least, she left a note.

I pad toward the bathroom but freeze in place when I glance toward the bedroom. It's dark, but I can make out a silhouetted form outlined on my bed and pause as I realize she's still here. I take a couple steps into the room, confirming it's not an illusion as I take in her golden hair strewn across my pillow, soft breaths gently leaving her in a light snore, and can't help the smile that I feel lifting my cheeks. *She stayed.* I run my fingers delicately over the soft strands of her hair and marvel a moment that she waited.

I turn and tip-toe to the bathroom and take a quick shower. I climb out, dry off, wrap the towel around my waist, and then notice that the clothes we were wearing earlier are folded neatly on the end of the counter. Treading as quietly as possible, I creep into the bedroom, find a pair of boxers and a t-shirt, and slip back out into the living area. I slide the clothes on and then sit on the couch for a minute. *Should I wake her up, climb into bed beside her, or wait here until she wakes?* I reach up, absently scratching the scruff on my face, when I notice her note on the table.

I pick it up and start reading and realize that it's not a note at all, but a poem? Or, maybe, the start of one?

> *a low-lit bar in the sunset heat*
> *voice that makes me stare in wonder*
> *crazy rhythm lingers and whiskey neat*
> *lightning strikes rumbles dark thunder*

HOLY SHIT. I DIGEST THE WORDS AGAIN. *THIS IS ABOUT HOW WE met.* The words are so simple but say so much. She told me she was a writer but didn't say what she wrote. Poems? Stories? It's a little love note. Another layer has bloomed, and my decision has been made.

I place the paper back on the table, rise, and walk quietly into the bedroom. I loom over the bed for a moment, gaining a bit of courage, then slide under the covers. She moans softly, turns to me, snuggles up against me like a kitten, and I wrap my arms around her. Her body is warm and her scent like roses as I inhale. I listen to the cadence of her breathing until it settles into a steady rhythm again, my eyes finally closing as I drift off.

I ROLL OVER AND INSTANTLY REALIZE THAT THE BED IS EMPTY. Quickly getting out of the bed, I move around the small cottage to see if she's in the living space or bathroom, but it's empty. I let out a sigh of disappointment as I glance at the clock. It's only five-thirty and still dark out. I wonder what time she left and worry because it had to have been pitch black out there. I slide my bare feet into my boots, grab a sweatshirt off a hook by the door, and walk outside in the direction of where her car was parked. I won't have a moment's peace until I at least know she made it to her car safely.

Stupid girl. Doesn't she know there are wolves out here sometimes? It's a farm, for crying out loud. They are always lingering around for the smaller stock and chickens. The sun is starting to show over the horizon, and I'm glad, as it's making the hike over to the main drive a little easier. I reach the knoll and can see now that her car is gone. I frown, disappointed that I didn't wake up with her in my arms. Turning, I head back to the house. I didn't even get her damn telephone number, so I can't even call her. *Now, who's the stupid one?*

I walk back inside the cottage and make myself a couple eggs and toast before heading to the bathroom to wash up and brush my teeth. I flip on the light and walk over to the sink, turning on the faucets. I glance up at the mirror and freeze, a huge smile breaking across my face. I read the message she's left for me in red lipstick and realize it's Saturday, and that means I'll be singing at Hook's Landing later. That means I'll be seeing her. The day just got a whole lot brighter.

See ya at the bar tonight, handsome!
XO Sydney

CHAPTER SEVEN

I try to roll over, and when I can't, my eyes fly open in panic. It lasts only a second as I realize Justin must have joined me sometime during the night and it's his arms that are holding me in place. He's breathing heavily, and I wonder how long he's been asleep. I relax against him and relish the feeling of being in his arms. But then my mind wanders to that kiss from earlier. Holy crap. That was the best first kiss of all first kisses ever. If his brother hadn't walked in, I'm not sure we would have stopped.

I reach up and trace my fingers over my lips, remembering the way his felt on mine. Warm and soft and perfect. That's what they felt like. I let out a long sigh. What am I doing? Even though he hasn't told me as much, Kelly mentioned that he's leaving at the end of the summer. Do I really want to do this to myself? I look up at his face, so relaxed, so beautiful even in sleep, and I find my answer. Yes. Why the hell not? Life is way too short not to take a chance every now and then.

But, that being the case, I also know that when he wakes up, if I'm still here, things are probably going to go to the next level way too quickly. And, even though I was pretty close to going there yesterday, I'm thinking a little more sensibly now that he's not kissing me. I slide myself slowly from his grasp and out of the bed. I walk softly to the bathroom and pull on my shorts but decide to leave his shirt on. After pulling my lipstick from my pocket and leaving him a note, I grab my sweater and boots and carry them outside, quietly shutting the front door behind me.

I pull on my boots and look up, realizing its pitch black out here. Of course, I left my cell in my car, so using the flashlight isn't an option. Biting my lip, I look out over the field, waiting for my eyes to adjust, and wonder if I can do this. It's dark and creepy, and I can hear things howling in the distance. I pull my big girl panties up, step off the porch, and decide to just walk really fast and look straight ahead. I mean, what's the worst that could happen? A big, bad wolf is going to come and get me?

I GLANCE AT THE DOOR AS IT SWINGS OPEN, FROWNING WHEN I SEE it's just one of our regulars, Joe, and not Justin. I look at the clock for about the twentieth time this afternoon, registering that it's only three-thirty, and shake my head. When he came in to set up last week, it was around this time, but there's no guarantee it's his regular time. I scold myself again for not remembering to leave him my number and having to go through this torture all afternoon of just waiting for him to show up. Because there is no way I am calling him.

I absently grab a Bud Lite from the cooler, twist off the cap, and slide it across the bar to Joe, my eyes glued to the door. "You waiting for someone, Syd?"

I swing my gaze to Joe, realize how rude I'm being, and offer him an apologetic smile. "Sorry, Joe. Just thinking about a couple things."

"Awful quiet in here today." He looks around and shrugs, disappointment evident in his voice.

"Well, it is the Saturday before Mother's Day. Maybe folks are out shopping." I wipe the counter down in front of him, the condensation from his beer leaving a small ring of water, and place a coaster under it. "Besides, it's still early. I'm sure things will liven up later."

"Yup." He grumbles. "I sure hope so. No fun drinking alone."

I smile and pull a five out of the tip jar and make my way under the bar. "Why don't I put some music on for us then, Joe? You got any requests?"

His eyes light up as I walk by, and he follows me over to the jukebox. "Oh, you know, I always love me some Johnny Cash, or you can't go wrong with some good ole Hank Williams."

"I know we've got "Ring of Fire" on here, but I don't think any Hank." I browse through the list of songs. "How about Kenny Rogers? We've got "The Gambler"?"

"Sure, sure! Kenny's great."

I punch in the numbers for the first two songs, and we continue to read through the song list, finding more and continuing to punch in numbers as the horn intro for "Ring of Fire," followed by Johnny's deep voice, fills the bar with music.

"I think we've got a good set picked out, Joe, but there are still a few more credits if you want to keep going." I point to the number, indicating six credits still left.

"Can I pick a song?" His voice sends shivers down my spine as it vibrates against my ear, and my pulse quickens as I feel him behind me. I was so busy picking out songs that I didn't even hear him come in. I pull my bottom lip between my teeth to try to lessen the smile that's blooming on my face. Before I can answer, I feel a strong hand on my hip and another snake around me to punch in a number, his front flush against my back. "I hear this song has a great rhythm."

I notice it's the number for "Linger," the song we danced to last weekend. "Music and rhythm find their way into the secret places of the soul," I whisper so I know only he will hear it. Joe seems to understand something is happening here and discreetly walks away. In the background, all I can hear is Johnny crooning about falling into a ring of fire, and for once, I completely understand what he's been singing about.

"More quotes? Who is it this time?" His hand is still on my waist, and the other is flat against the jukebox. I'm a prisoner, but I don't mind one bit.

"It's Plato."

"God, you're so damn smart." He chuckles, and I feel his nose brush against my hair, which I wore down since I know he likes it that way, and then across my cheek before his warm lips brush the softest kiss across mine.

He steps back then, leaving my back feeling cold but igniting my insides, and I turn slowly to look at him. "Hi."

"Hi." His gaze travels over me and he nods. "You look pretty."

"Do I?" I smile shyly and swipe my hands over the olive-green t-shirt dress I'm wearing. I threw a wide, braided belt around the waist and have my boots on. It's way dressier than I usually wear to the bar, but I wanted to look nice for him, not that I'm going to tell him that. "Thanks."

"The color makes your eyes look greener." He reaches up and lifts my chin a fraction and gazes into them.

I can feel my cheeks heating, so I take a step back and motion toward the bar. "I should get back to work."

He nods and his mouth dips into a slight smirk. "At least, this time, you're letting me know you're leaving."

I grimace and step toward him. "Are you angry? I'm sorry! I just didn't want to wake you. I had no idea what time you came in."

His hand reaches out and glides gently down my arm before lightly grasping my hand. "Not mad. Worried." He shakes his head and gives me a grin that's just a shade shy of being wicked. "There are wolves roaming around out there. What if one of them had got you?"

I WATCH HER WALK AWAY, APPRECIATING THE WAY HER HIPS ROCK back and forth until she pulls herself under and through the bar. My cheeks are getting sore from all the smiling I've done over the last twenty-four hours, but I just can't seem to stop. I turn and set up my equipment as quickly as I can because I want to get a few minutes in at the bar with her before I have to go back to the barn. I notice Kelly doesn't seem to be around and wonder where she is.

I look over my shoulder to take in the room and see who else is around and, when I do, catch her watching me. I wink, but she looks away before I can catch her eye. She's shy as a church mouse, and I chuckle, hoping she won't have to resort to shots again tonight. I thought she was getting a bit more comfortable with me, but maybe not. I plug in the last speaker and make my way over to my usual stool and sit down. "Where's Kelly?"

"Oh, she'll be in later. She and Adam had an appointment with the minister today about their wedding. They're getting married in October."

"The cop who came in last week? Big guy?"

She smiles and nods. "That would be him. He's a good guy. First guy I've ever seen that can keep Kelly in line."

"What about you?"

"What about me?"

"Ever had a guy that kept you in line?" As soon as I say the words, I realize how stupid I sound, and it's not just the expression on her face right now. "Oh, Jesus, I didn't mean it like that! That was my stupid way of asking about old boyfriends."

"Uh-huh." She's nodding her head, but her expression still looks like she wants to maybe smack me. "You want something to drink, Justin?"

"Ice water?" I say meekly.

"Feeling a little bit like you're in Hell right now?" Then she bursts out laughing, breaking the awkwardness of the moment just like that, and I know then and there that all I want is to spend more time with her.

"So, are you going to let me take you on a real date this time?" I watch her as she fills a glass with ice then water and places it in front of me, her eyes finally darting up to look at me, her lower lip clenched in her teeth. "I could take you to dinner tomorrow?"

She releases her lip and her brow furrows. "But it's Mother's Day. Won't you want to do something with your mom?"

"We always do a special lunch with my mom and grandmother, so my night's free." I shrug, and then it hits me. "Oh, jeez, sorry. You probably have plans with your mom, though, huh?"

I watch as her face changes completely. Her eyes blink rapidly to keep tears at bay, and her lips turn downward as she shakes her head then clears her throat. "My mom died six years ago. I go visit her stone in the morning, but otherwise, I'm free."

"Oh, shit." I don't know what else to do, so I get up, walk to the cut-through, squeeze under, and then go to her and wrap her in my arms. "I'm sorry. I didn't know."

Her arms find their way around my waist as she muffles into my chest. "How could you have?"

"I don't know, but I'm still sorry." I pull her closer, trying to hug away some of the pain she's feeling and because, honestly, I don't know what else to do.

After a minute, she pushes apart from me and shrugs, her

cheeks pink. "I'm sorry. I'm usually fine to talk about it, but sometimes, like the day before Mother's Day, it hits me a little harder."

"Hey, don't apologize for that." I place my hand on her cheek and, without thinking, bend down and kiss her. Not a long or passionate kiss, just a simple touch to try to let her feel something else right now. Her eyes meet mine, and when she gives me a lopsided smile, I know it's her way of telling me she's okay. I let my hand fall and nod before making my back to the other side of the bar.

"Do you want to talk about it? Does it make it better or worse?" I take a sip of my water to help calm my nerves. I've never really spoken to anyone about death or had anyone close to me die, so I'm not sure what I should do.

She gives me a small smile, her eyes sad, and shrugs. "It is what it is. She got cancer. She fought really, really hard, but she lost. I miss her. I miss her a lot. But I know she's around and with me, so I just try to take some comfort in that."

"What about your dad?" I ask quietly.

"He's still here but not the same since he lost her." I watch as she picks at one of the coasters. "I try to go seem him once or twice a month, and he comes into the library every so often to visit. He lives here in town still."

"Sydney, I'm really sorry. I can't imagine." I take her hand and squeeze it, thinking of my mom and how lost and empty my life would seem without her.

She gives my hand a squeeze back and then looks shyly up at me through her lashes. "I would actually like to go out tomorrow if the offer is still good? It would be a really nice way to spend what might otherwise be a shitty day for me, ya know?"

The corners of my mouth slide up and I nod. "I'd love to try to make it a better day for you." I let go of her hand and grab a cocktail napkin off a stack on the bar then slide it over to her. "How about you give me your number this time?"

Her eyes crinkle in delight as she grabs a pen off the counter, quickly jots her number on the napkin, and slides it back to me. "Oh, wait!" She grabs it back and writes something under her number, then gives it back to me. "That's my address. You can pick me up at six."

I grin widely, slide the napkin in my pocket, and rise to leave. "It's a date."

CHAPTER EIGHT

I stand in front of the mirror with a frown, assessing the fifth outfit I've now tried on. I'm wearing a cute pair of black satin shorts with a sleeveless white top, but I'm not sure how the weather will be later and don't want to get too chilly. I pull on a jean jacket to see how it looks but wonder if it's too casual now. *Where's Kelly when I need her?* Justin is going to be here in thirty minutes so I need to make a decision and fast.

I walk back over to my bed and pick up my black rayon jumper pants. Deciding they will be the perfect compromise, I smile. I slide the shorts off and the pants on, and then walk back over to the mirror and look at myself one more time. I slide the jacket off and decide I'll just carry it with me and wear it if I need it. Mission complete. *Who knew getting ready for a date could be so difficult?*

Hair and make-up done, I pull my shoes on then walk out into the kitchen and open the fridge to see what I have to drink. I spy a bottle of white wine I haven't opened yet and pull that out. After twisting it open, I pull a glass down from the shelf, fill it halfway, and then go to the living room and take a seat on the couch to wait. Simba, my big, orange fluff ball of a cat, saunters out of my bedroom and jumps up beside me.

"Hey, my little man. Coming to give me some love?" I stroke his fur and he immediately starts purring. I laugh at just how loud this cat's motor is when he purrs. I've never heard another cat like him. He really is my little lion. I take a sip of my wine, moving my attention away from him for one moment, which results in a head-butt to my leg and a coating of orange cat fur on my black pants. "Oh, Simba, what am I going to do with you, you little ball of fur?"

I rise, give him a final pat, and move to the kitchen to see if I can find my lint brush. I open drawer after drawer, but of course, the time when I need it the most, I can't find it. Seriously, Murphy's Law is in full effect. Desperate times call for desperate measures, so I grab the duct tape I keep for emergencies just like this and rip off a big piece. I stick the two ends together, slide the smooth part over my hand, and pat the sticky side over my pants, successfully picking off all Simba's hair. I smile and congratulate myself on a job well done by taking a big sip of my wine, just as a loud knock sounds at the door. I jump and almost spill wine down the front of my shirt, but somehow manage to keep it in the glass. *Gah! He's here!*

After setting the glass on the counter, I walk quickly to the door, yank it open, and have to stop myself from gaping when I see Justin. Instead of the jeans I'm used to seeing him in, he's wearing black dress pants and a white button-down shirt with the sleeves rolled up and the collar open just enough that I can see a peek of his chest. His black belt matches the sharp, black dress shoes he's wearing, completing his look. "Hi. Do you want to come in?"

Instead of an answer, the smile on his face transforms into a look of surprise, and he laughs, then slaps his hand over his mouth as he tries to stop. "I'm sorry. I swear, I'm not laughing at you!"

I look up and down my body, to see if I did actually spill wine on myself, trying to figure out what he's laughing at. "What? Justin, tell me!"

He steps in, taking my arm by the elbow, and leans down to

kiss me on the cheek. "First, I just want to say that you look really nice. Beautiful, in fact."

"Okay..." My brows are furrowed and eyes crinkled as I continue to wonder what the hell is so funny.

"Look at us." He points to himself and then me. "We look like wait staff in our matching outfits."

I look at him and then at me, and then back at him again, and realize he's absolutely correct. Laughing, I bring my hands to my face. "Oh my God! You're right! We look ridiculous!"

"No, no!" He's trying so hard not to laugh. "Seriously, you look amazing, but this is just too funny."

"There is no way I'm going to dinner looking like twins." I hold my finger out. "I'll be right back." I point to the fridge. "There's wine in there and glasses on that shelf. Just help yourself."

I run through the bathroom, to my bedroom on the other side, and find the pink shirt I tried earlier. It's only a little wrinkled from being tossed in the discard pile, but it will do. I pull the white shirt off, pull the pink one on, and run my hands over it to try to smooth out the creases. I shake my head. It's just going to have to do. As I walk back to the bathroom, I check my reflection, fluff my hair, and give myself a thumbs up.

"Okay, better?" I stroll out of the bathroom into the kitchen and spin around, finding him sitting on the couch with Simba in his lap. "Oh no!" I frown. "He's going to get fur all over you!"

"This is nothing compared to what I get on me at the farm." I watch as he continues to run his hand down and over the cat, and I think I might actually be a little bit jealous but also a little bit smitten that he could care less about the hair. "And you still look amazing, in pink or in white."

"Yeah, well, at least now we won't be mistaken for the wonder twins, or worse, the help." I giggle and motion for him to get up. "Come on, I'll treat you to my special pet hair removal system." I rip him his very own piece of duct tape and help him brush the fur off his pants.

"If you keep doing that, we're never going to make it to dinner." I look up at him, surprised by the look of heat that's flaring in his eyes, and immediately step away.

"Sorry." I grin sheepishly and pull the tape from my hand. "I'm ready if you are."

His gaze doesn't leave mine as he responds, his voice a bit gravely. "Yep, I'm ready."

"Dinner, Justin. I'm ready to go to dinner," I respond, making sure we're talking about the same thing.

He smiles wickedly. "Can't blame a guy for trying." He gives me a playful wink and chuckles. "Do you have everything you need?"

I grab my jacket and purse then nod. "I'm good."

"Okay, let's go. I made reservations for us at Tilton's. Have you been?"

I raise my brows in appreciation. Tilton's is one of the nicer restaurants in the area. "Not in a long time."

We leave the house, and he waits as I lock my door. Taking my hand, he walks me to his truck and helps me in. I'm not sure why, but I didn't picture him having a truck. I know he works on a farm, but I pictured him as the muscle car, musician kind of guy more than a farmer kind of guy. He moves around to the driver's side, jumps in, and starts up the engine. "All set?"

I nod my head, excited to be spending some time with him, and smile brightly. "All set."

I look over and hope she's okay riding in the truck. She drives a little compact car, and she's all dressed up wearing heels. "I hope the truck's okay. I almost took my mom's car instead, but I just feel more comfortable driving this."

"Of course, I'm okay." She looks at me, her eyes wide. "Why wouldn't I be? This is a great truck."

"I don't know. You're all dressed up, and I'm taking you on a date, and you're maybe looking too pretty to be in a truck."

She scoffs. "Justin, don't be silly. The truck is fine. Don't forget, I'm just a small-town girl. Nothing special about me."

"Well, I'll hope you'll let me be the judge of that. I might have a different opinion on the matter." I look over at her and smile when I see her cheeks are flushed with color again. It takes about twenty-five minutes to get to the restaurant, but the time flies as we easily fall into conversation about how busy the night before was at the bar, how lunch went with my mom and grandmother, and how many more new calves have been born since she visited. "We named Maisy's new calf after you since she seemed to take quite a liking to you."

"Shut up!" She slaps me playfully on the arm. "You did not name a cow after me!"

"We did. She's our very first Sydney. You're gonna have to come and see her."

"Oh my gosh, I totally will." I'm thrilled to see her face light up with delight over such a simple thing. "Just let me know when."

I park the truck, shut the engine off, and jump out so I can go around and help her down. She's already trying to step out when I get to her side, so I reach out and wrap my hands around her waist to help lower her down. As her feet touch the ground, she looks up at me, that damn lip in her teeth again, and just stares at me for a moment. Her hands are over mine, and I can feel her pulse quicken when I pull her in just a little closer and lean in and whisper in her ear. "I really, really want to kiss you again."

Her head tilts so she can look me in the eye as she whispers back, "But?"

I grin mischievously. "But then we may never make it to dinner, and I'm hungry." Instead, I place my lips on hers for the briefest of moments, so I can get just a little taste and then pull away, her eyes following me. "Come on, let's go in."

I take her hand, pull her away from the truck, and then shut the door before leading her inside the restaurant. They seat us at a quiet table next to a window overlooking the street, and we both agree it's perfect for people watching. We order wine, and I'm ecstatic that she's not one of those girls that orders a salad and then just picks at it. She orders a rib eye and mashed potatoes and actually eats it.

During dinner, we talk about how college was for her, and how not going to college was for me. We talk about how books feed her soul and about the story ideas she has floating around in her head. I tell her it's exactly how I feel about music and writing songs. She finally tells me more about what she writes, even confessing that she recently sent a book she finished this winter off to several publishers and that she goes to the mailbox every day checking for a reply.

The more we talk, the more connected I feel to her, and the guiltier I begin to feel knowing I'm leaving in the fall. I don't want to lead her on, but since I'm not really sure I even know where this is going yet, I don't know if I should say anything. I watch as she takes another sip of her wine, her delicate lips on the edge of the glass, and know this is a girl I don't want to be unfair to. I need to be upfront with her, so I take a deep breath and blow it out before I begin.

"So, just to be fair, you should know I'll be leaving for New York in the fall." I watch her set the wine glass on the table and nod her head.

"Yeah, Kelly mentioned you said something to her about that."

Her fingers trail around the base of the glass as she continues. "So, it's a sure thing then that you're going?"

"I leave in September. I've been planning and saving up for the last two years. I have a friend with a small record company in Brooklyn. We're going to make a demo album and try to get it out to some of the big labels."

She takes a sip of her wine and looks up at me with a small smile on her face. "It's a good plan, and you are so talented. I'd hate to see you waste that here in a small town."

"It's all I've ever dreamed of. My whole life, for as long as I can remember, all I've ever wanted to do is play my music to thousands of people."

"Then you're doing the right thing. You have to follow your dreams, Justin." Her smile is genuine, but I can also see a sadness in her eyes.

"The problem is, now that I've met you, and now that I'm getting to know you, I don't want to stop."

"Who says we have to?" She shrugs lightly. "I mean, do we have to have a bunch of rules around this? If we like spending time together, can't we just do that then? Whatever happens, happens. I mean, it's only May. September is a whole season away."

Is this girl for real? My mouth almost hangs open in shock at how easy going she's being about this. "Seriously?"

She laughs softly. "Seriously. I mean, who knows? By July, you may end up running away with Sheila."

My eyes fly open in surprise. "Sheila from the pub? The one Kelly calls Bozo the Clown, Sheila?"

She laughs out loud and then covers her mouth when she realizes everyone in the restaurant has turned to look at her. "Well, she is your biggest fan."

"Oof. I think I'll stick with you if that's okay."

She smiles sweetly at me and finally responds, her voice quiet. "That's okay with me."

MICHELLE WINDSOR

CHAPTER NINE

*H*e pays the check, helps me put my coat on, and leads me back to the truck to take me home. We're both quiet for a few minutes; I think both of us are digesting our dinner and the conversation we just had. When I can't stand it any longer, I reach out and motion to his radio. "Okay if I turn it on?"

He nods. "Sure."

I push the power button on and turn to look at him as soon as the music pours over the speakers. The song "Linger" is playing, and I wonder to myself if this is a damn sign. Before I can even ask, he reaches for the eject button and pushes it, a Cranberries disc sliding out. He takes it, slips it into a pocket on his visor, then looks at my stunned expression and shrugs. "What? I like that song."

I feel my cheeks lift and nod back at him. "It's recently become a favorite of mine, too." I unbuckle my seatbelt and slide closer to him so I can see what other CDs he might have hidden in his visor when the truck comes to a screeching halt. His arm is out and holding me in place, keeping me from flying forward as I clutch the dash.

"You okay?" He looks over at me and then back at the road. I nod my head, tongue-tied and still in shock at the abrupt stop. "Look." He points out the window. "There are baby foxes in the road."

I look out the window, and sure enough, there are three little babies in the middle of the road surrounding something. "Is that their mom? Is she dead?"

"I'm not sure." I watch as he flips the hazards on and hops out of the truck. "Stay put while I check it out."

Well, that's not going to happen! I open my door, climb out of my side, and sneak around the front of the truck where he's crouched down and investigating. His head pops up when he sees me, and a frown appears on his lips before he looks back down at the foxes. "It looks like one of the babies got run over and they don't want to leave it."

I scoot closer, but slowly so I don't scare the little ones away. "Is it alive? Can we do anything for it? Do you think the mom is around?"

He shakes his head. "No, it's definitely gone. The mom's probably not far away, but she's smart enough to stay out of the road." He reaches up and runs his hand through his neat hair and sighs. "I think the only thing I can do is move the dead one off into the woods and hope the little ones will follow. At least we can get them out of the road that way."

I nod my head at his plan. "Okay, what can I do? Anything?"

He points to the truck. "Can you grab my work gloves out of the side pocket in the driver's door?"

I run around him and the foxes over to the door, grab the gloves, and then run back and hand them to him. I can't believe no cars have come by yet. I guess it's one of the advantages to Sunday night in a small town. I watch him pull the gloves on and then gently push the little foxes away from their dead sibling as he scoops it up. He carries it over to the side of the road, walks about ten feet into the woods, and sets it down.

I'm so happy when I see the other little ones actually follow behind him and scurry into the woods and off the road. He walks out of the woods, clapping the gloves together to loosen away any of the fur and grime, and I run up to him and throw my arms around him in a hug.

"That was so amazing!" I kiss him quickly on the cheek and step back. "You're their hero!"

He grins sheepishly and puts an arm around me to lead me back to the truck. "I couldn't leave them in the road to get run over."

"Many would have driven right by." I beam up at him, feeling like he saved my life and not the foxes', and think I might be falling just a little bit in love with him right here.

"Come on, up you go." He lifts me up into the truck on the driver's side and then slides in next to me. I stay in the middle, wanting to be close to him, and rest my hand on his leg as he starts the truck and continues the drive back to my house.

His rests his hand over mine, and I shiver each time his thumb runs back and forth against my skin. We're both quiet, both stealing looks at each other, both feeling something more building. When we finally get to my apartment, he jumps out, pulls me across the seat, and wraps his hands around my waist to lower me to the ground. I look up at him as he lowers me and, for the first time, notice how dark his eyes look. He takes my hand and leads me up the stairs. "Come on."

At the top, I dig my keys out of my purse and unlock the door. I step inside first, and he follows, shutting the door and then pressing me up against it as his lips slam against mine. I drop my purse and keys to the ground and wrap my arms around his neck, gripping onto his hair as his hands find my face. His tongue sweeps across my lips, and I moan, giving him the invitation to explore further with his tongue, our teeth clacking as we cling to each other almost desperately.

His hands slide down my body and under my legs, lifting them, urging me to wrap them around his waist, and he grinds into me.

The sensation against my core causes me to moan, my head thrusting back and slamming into the door. "Ouch." I reach up and rub the back of my head, and he swings us away from the door, walking the short distance to the couch.

He spins again, sitting down, my legs shifting so I'm straddling him, his hand moving to my back, pulling me flush to him. "Better?"

"Better." I fuse my mouth to his, and we are all tongues and hot breaths and moans as I rub my core over his hardened length, his hand tangled in my hair. I'm so hot and move to take my jacket off, which he helps me with once he realizes what I'm doing. Next, he's pulling my shirt over my head, his eyes fixed on my lace-covered breasts once it's off. I pull back slightly and begin unbuttoning his shirt as quickly as I can, pulling on the tucked in portion until it comes free of his pants and then slide it over his shoulders and off his arms.

I run my hands over the smooth planes of his chest, down his bumpy abdomen, and then back up again, finally resting them on his shoulders. He's so Goddamn beautiful in his perfection that I just want to run my hands over every inch of him. I push against his shoulders and then stand up, looking down at him, his brows furrowed and head tilted in question.

I hold my hand out. "Come with me."

Taking her hand, I stand, thanking the heavens above that she isn't telling me no. I follow her as she walks through the bathroom, which leads to her bedroom. I chuckle as she drops my hand and moves to the bed, quickly scooping up a pile of clothes and moving them to a chair in the corner of the room. "Sorry. I can be a bit of a slob."

I nod my head, move to stand in front of her, and then bring my fingers to the tie holding her pants up. "Why don't we add these to that pile over there?" As I lower my lips to hers, I untie the knot. They slide to the floor, and she steps out of them as I move my hands to my own belt, making quick work of it and my button, before shoving them down my legs. I don't want to stop kissing her, so I toe my shoes off and then step out of my pants as I push her down onto the bed.

Lowering myself over her until I feel her skin against mine, I slowly thrust myself against her, my cock straining against my briefs. Her back arches off the bed, her covered breasts rubbing into my chest as her hands clutch against my back, her nails digging in. Sliding my hand down over her breast, I feel her hardened nipple and continue down, slipping it between us until my fingers brush the elastic of her underwear.

My hand glides under the fabric and then lower until I feel her core under my fingers. I drag my finger through her wetness, eliciting a long moan as her hips surge forward at my touch. I continue rubbing as I kiss her neck and then suck on a taut nipple through the material of her bra. Her hand moves over my cock, grabbing it and then squeezing, and I groan loudly.

"Condom? Do you have a condom?" she asks between heavy breaths, and I nod my head, reaching on the floor and into my pants pocket for my wallet. I pull the condom out with my teeth, and she grabs it, ripping the packet open and handing it back to me, then moves to push my briefs down over my hips. I roll to my side and slide the condom on as she pushes her own underwear down and off her legs.

I roll back over and lower myself slowly, finding her gaze before moving any further. "Are you sure?"

"Oh my God, yes." Her hands find my ass, and she moves me between her legs in desperation. I line myself up to her core and push the tip in slowly. I want to keep my eyes open so I can see her face, but she feels so Goddamn good that they close in ecstasy as her core tightens around me. When I'm all the way in, I stay still for just a moment, savoring the feeling of her pulsing around my cock, and then pull out and surge back in.

"God! Justin, that feels so good!" She's clutching my back, meeting me thrust for thrust, as I continue to move in and out of her. I grip the pillow under her head, bringing her face to mine, and kiss her. I want to feel every piece of her.

I move over her and change my rhythm, grinding my hips against her, feeling myself rub against her clit. She grips me harder, her mouth falling open. Her eyes scrunch up. "Oh, I'm going to come. I'm going to come."

Thrusting harder, I grab her hair in my hands now, pulling her head back as I push in one last time, exploding as I feel her insides clench onto my cock in a tight grip, before pulsing madly. "Fuck, you're so perfect, so fucking perfect."

I loosen my grip on her hair and look down at her as I feel her grip on my back relax and the muscles locked around my cock soften. Her eyes flutter open, her lashes brushing against her flushed cheeks as she blinks, her lips puffy from our kissing. I lean down and brush my lips lightly against them as I slowly pull out of her and roll over.

I roll the condom off and then carry it to the toilet and flush it away. When I walk quickly back to the bed, I notice her eyes are following my every move. "What are you looking at?"

"Just your fine ass." She giggles. "I mean, I've always thought it looked pretty good in your jeans, but damn, it's even better in the flesh."

I slide my boxers on, find her underwear on the floor and hand them to her, and then slide back in the bed next to her. She wiggles the lacy panties on and then lays across my chest, her blonde hair spilling across it like a blanket. I run my fingers through it, loving how silky it feels against my skin. "That was pretty amazing."

"Uh-huh." Even from here, I can see her cheeks flushing pink. "Definitely amazing."

"Who knew foxes were such a turn-on?" I chuckle, her head bobbing under the movement.

"It wasn't the foxes. It's what you did with the foxes." She turns her head toward me and raises her eyebrows. "Seriously hot."

"Really? Saving a few foxes?" I shrug, not sure what to think. I deal with animals all day long so it doesn't really seem like a big deal to me.

"Justin, you sing beautifully, you're a gentleman, you are insanely good looking, seem to be fairly smart, and now you saved some wildlife. If a girl's panties don't get wet over that, there's a problem."

"You think I'm insanely good looking?" I smile, getting slightly full of myself.

She rolls over and climbs up my body, finally resting in a straddled position over me. She brings a finger up to my lips and runs it slowly down the center of my body, not stopping until she's reached the juncture between her legs. "Do you want to see what your insanely good looks are doing to *my* panties?"

Holy fucking shit. She's a completely different person in bed. A complete wildcat. I grin wickedly and then roll over, pinning her under me, and slide down to find out just how good looking she thinks I am.

CHAPTER TEN

It's only been three weeks since Justin took me to dinner at Tilton's, but it seems like so much more time has passed between us. We spend almost every night together; me mostly at his place because he has to get up so early to work the farm. But on weekends, he's been staying with me since I live closer to the bar.

Every weekend, Justin is bringing a bigger crowd into the bar, so big that we had to actually hire a door person to manage the crowd. It's been great for me and Kelly, since the tips are rolling in, and we started charging a cover that we split with Justin. I still haven't heard back from any of the publishing houses I sent my book to, but I keep checking the mail each day, hoping sooner or later I'll get some news.

It's Wednesday, and just after two-thirty, so I'm at the library, putting away the books Mr. Arnold used today. I have no idea what that man is researching. He tells me it's a secret project and I'll know what I need to know when I need to know it. Kids are still in school for another week, but with finals done and out of the way, I don't expect things to get any busier today.

The door swishes, and I look up, my lips curving into a smile as a thousand butterflies flutter in my stomach when Justin strolls toward me. "Hey, beautiful."

I come around the table and meet him halfway. "Hey yourself." He wraps me in his arms and brings his lips to mine, their warmth always welcome. After a minute, I push him away, my body heating, and fan myself. "You sure know how to kiss a girl."

He beams and plants his hands on my waist then walks me backward until we're in the far corner, pushing me up against one of the stacks. "I know how to do a few other things, too." He waggles his brows and bends down, planting soft kisses along my neck and up to my ear.

"Hmmm, that feels nice." I run my fingers through his thick locks and close my eyes, my skin pebbling even though I'm feeling warmer. His lips stop, and I open my eyes to find him looking at my hair. "What?"

"Why do you always have that pencil stuck in there?" He motions to the top of my head with his chin because his hands are currently busy rubbing my ass.

"My hair always gets in my eyes when I'm reading, so I knot it up on top of my head and throw a pencil in to hold it. Does it bother you?" I pat my hair with my hand, trying to find the damn pencil.

He shakes his head and gives me a feral grin. "I love it, especially when you wear these tight skirts. It's sexy as hell."

I finally find the pencil and pull it out, my hair tumbling down around my face in waves as I shake my head slightly, and then pull my bottom lip between my teeth, knowing full well what that does to him.

He growls softly, leans in, and sucks my lip from my teeth. "This works, too." Then, he crashes his mouth to mine, his hands clenching onto my skirt, pulling it slowly up to expose my legs. His fingers drag slowly over my skin to my inner thigh and keep moving north until they brush against the silk of my panties.

His lips leave my mouth, his breathing heavy as he pants into my ear. "Jesus, Sydney, you're so wet."

He drags his fingers heavily across my swollen clit, and I push into his hand as I moan. "Your fault. Too good looking." I whimper and bite his shoulder when he slips a finger under the material and pushes it into my center. I feel myself throb around him and push down, wanting so much more.

"You're so fucking hot, Sydney." He takes my hand and moves it to his hard, hard length. "Look what you do to me." He nips my neck and sucks hard when I grip him and squeeze, still grinding into his hand.

"I'm going to come if you keep doing that." I wither under his touch, wanting and not wanting it at the same time. We're in the library for God's sakes!

He runs his tongue up my throat and bites gently on my lobe, thrusting another finger in as he does, my legs almost giving out under me. "Good. I love watching you come. You look so gorgeous when you do."

I mewl as he uses his thumb to rub my clit in combination with the thrusting, and then bite down hard on his shoulder again as my body quakes around him. My legs turn to jelly under me, and I feel his other arm wrap around my waist and hold me up as I shatter, sparks flying in a thousand bright shards behind my clenched eyes. His lips seal over mine, kissing me until the world spins back into place. "Oh my God, Justin. How do you do that every time?"

He peppers small kisses over my cheeks, my nose, and my lips, as his hand slides from between my legs and then up to his mouth where he inserts two fingers and sucks, his eyes closing in satisfaction. Just watching him do this gets my pulse racing again, and I trail my hand over his hard length, pressing as I go. He groans and pulls his fingers from his mouth, pressing it back over mine, his tongue sweeping across my lips, the taste of me still lingering.

I bring my hand to the button of his jeans, pop it open, and begin sliding the zipper open...

"Hello? Is anyone here?" A deep, male voice freezes us both in place.

"Shit!" I whisper and push Justin off of me, pulling my skirt down and back into place. I run my hands over the rest of myself and try to smooth down my hair. "How do I look?"

"Like you just came all over my hand," he drawls out, a content smile spread across his face.

"Just one second!" I flash a scowl at him. "Just putting something away back here!"

"Yeah, my cock." He chuckles at his own joke but then stops when he sees the worry on my face. "What's the big deal?"

I stomp my foot and then turn and hurry down the length of the stacks and out of the corner into the main library. "Hey, Dad! You didn't tell me you were coming by today."

DAD? FUUCCK! I FASTEN THE BUTTON OF MY JEANS, MY COCK immediately soft. After making sure my shirt is tucked in, I grab the first book I see off the shelf. I follow after Sydney and hold the book up. "Here it is, Syd! Found it!"

She spins around, her face flushed, and grimaces, her eyes flying wide for just a moment as she mouths silently, "thanks", and grabs the book from my hand. "Perfect! Thanks, Justin."

She twirls back around, book in hand, and walks to her dad, giving him a hug and a kiss on the cheek. "This is a nice surprise."

He kisses her back. "Oh, I had to go down to the hardware store to pick up some bird seed, so thought I'd stop by while I was in town." His eyes travel in my direction and lock on me, and I immediately feel like I'm under a microscope. "Who's this?"

She turns her head toward me and then motions for me to come closer. "Dad, this is my friend, Justin. His parents own the big farm over on County Road. You know, the one with all the cows?"

I watch as he takes me in, his eyes raking me over from head to toe, a hard glint present as he nods. "Yup, I know the farm. Your dad Tom? Tom Jeffries?"

I take a step closer and nod my head. "Yes, sir, that's him. I'm his oldest son, Justin." I hold my hand out to him, and then cringe when he grasps it, remembering that less than ten minutes ago, it was rubbing against his daughter's private parts. My face heats as my pulse speeds up, and I pray he doesn't notice my palms are beginning to sweat.

"Yup, I played ball against your old man back in the day. He was a hell of a pitcher." He lets go of my hand and shakes his head. "Probably could've gone pro if he didn't have to work that damn farm for his father."

I always knew my dad had played ball but didn't realize he was that good, nor did I ever hear that taking over the farm was a sacrifice to him. I'll have to ask my mom about that. "Not sure about that, sir, but I do know he still likes to throw the ball around with me and my brother from time to time."

"Dad, did you need anything specific or are you just stopping in?" Sydney's voice is a little shaky, and she keeps shifting back and forth from one foot to another like she's getting ready to run.

"Oh, no, just wanted to stop in and see my girl." He pats her gently on the arm and then wraps it around her in a half hug. "You gonna come up and see me one of these weekends for dinner? It's been awhile."

"I know, Dad. I'm sorry. I've been really busy the last few weeks." Her eyes dart to me, and I look away, not wanting to feel any guiltier. "How about I stop over Saturday for lunch before my shift at Hook's? I can make lasagna for you?"

"Now, that sounds good." He smiles brightly and rubs his

stomach. "You know I love it when you make your mom's lasagna."

"Great!" She steps closer to him, hooks her arm through his, and leads him toward the exit. "It's a date."

He pulls her to a stop and turns to look at me and then back at her. "You can bring him, too, if you want. Looks like maybe I should be getting to know him a little better, eh?"

Her face turns five different shades of red in a matter of seconds as she tugs him away again. "Dad! Don't be rude!"

"How am I being rude? I'm telling him to come to lunch."

She gives him one more kiss on the cheek and pushes him out the door. "Bye, Dad. See you Saturday." She watches him exit before leaning her back against the door and banging her head against it lightly.

I rush up behind her and pull her away, turning her into my arms. "Hey, it wasn't that bad."

Her head arches up, wide eyes staring, her lips turned down. "Not that bad? Justin, he almost caught me giving you a hand job! How much worse does it have to get before it's bad?"

She clunks her head against my chest and lets out a pathetic moan. I chuckle, push my finger under her chin, and tilt her face back up. Brushing a light kiss across her lips, I try to ease her worries. "It was fine. I don't think he suspected a thing."

"Well, he definitely seems to think we're a thing!" She pushes out of my arms, stalks over to the desk on the other side of the room, and plops down on the stool.

I make my way over slowly and lean over the counter across from her. "Aren't we?"

"Aren't we what?" She blows out a puff of air, trying to move a piece of hair hanging in her face, and then gives up, gathering it in her hands before knotting it on top of her head and stabbing a pencil through its center. So sexy, and she doesn't even know it.

"Aren't we a thing?" I frown, surprised that I even have to ask the question. It's new territory for me. I don't usually put a label on any of the girls I'm with because they don't usually hang around longer than a few rolls in the sack.

"Don't you know, Justin?" She smiles coyly at me and tilts her head suggestively.

"Know what?" I ask tentatively, not sure where this is going.

"I let all the hot, local musicians take me in the stacks and have their way with me. Why ever would you think that means we're a thing?" She bats her eyelashes and pushes her lips into a slight pout.

"Why, Ms. Porter, are you telling me that you're one of *those* librarians? And here I was thinking you were something special." I grin roguishly and watch as she slides off the stool and walks back around the desk to where I'm standing. I turn to face her, my back leaning against the desk, my brows lifting when she comes to rest between my legs.

"Oh, you're something special all right, Mr. Jeffries." She stretches up on her tip-toes, placing her hands flat on my chest. Her tongue darts out, licking along my bottom lip, before she bites it gently. "I'll be more than happy to show you later just how special you are."

I smack her lightly on the ass, holding on once my palm lands there, and pull her closer to me. Fusing my lips to hers, I seal them tightly as I kiss her deeply. When I release her, she's breathing heavily and looks up at me, her eyes hooded. "You're my thing, Syd. Just to be clear."

"I like being your thing." Her teeth capture her lower lip as she tries to hide a smile.

I kiss her one more time for good measure and smile. "Well, good. Glad that's settled 'cause I have to get back to the farm."

She steps back out of my arms and sighs. "Okay, so, I'll see you later then?"

I pull her in for one more kiss and give her a nod as I back out of the room. "Can't wait. I wanna find out just how special I am." I throw her a playful wink and push out the door, her laughter echoing behind me as I go.

CHAPTER ELEVEN

*I*t's just after three-thirty when Justin and I push through the entrance to Hook's carrying his equipment for his gig that night. The cool air feels so good after spending the last three hours at my dad's house, who incidentally refuses to turn the air conditioner on unless it's over ninety degrees. It's eighty-eight, by the way, and I was in a kitchen with a hot oven on for half of the time. I feel like a sweaty mess. "I'm going to go clean-up a bit, okay?"

I give him a quick peck on the lips and slip under the bar and through the doors to the kitchen. "Hey, Kell!"

She looks up from the lemons she's cutting and gives me a smile. "Hey there, stranger. Please, don't tell me you're all flushed from having even more wild sex with that walking sex on a stick out there?"

I giggle and throw a lemon at her. "I wish! I was at Dad's cooking him Mom's lasagna, and of course, he refused to turn on the air. I feel like a hot, sticky bun right now."

"I've got a couple clean shirts in the back if you want to go wash up and borrow one."

"Yes! I was praying you had some here. I didn't want to have to run home, and Justin and I came in his truck, so it would have been a pain."

"Wait, one vehicle?" She sets the knife down on the table and raises a single brow at me. "Did he go to your dad's with you?"

"Uh-huh." I nod my head, knowing what's coming next.

"Syd! You've never brought anyone to meet your dad!" It comes out like a squeal, and I seriously think every person sitting in the bar had to have just heard her.

"Kelly, shhhh!" I giggle and quickly tell her what happened in the library and how my dad definitely knew something was up.

"So, was dinner good? Is Justin still alive?" She's moved on to cutting limes now but is completely engrossed in knowing every little detail of my life.

"It went really well. I can't believe it." I think back to the last few hours we spent at my dad's and still feel a bit surprised by how easily my dad and Justin seemed to hit it off. I think my dad was thrilled to finally have someone debate baseball with him, and of course, the lasagna was a hit.

"Hello?" Kelly and I both turn our heads toward the kitchen doors as Justin comes strolling through. "Ah, now this is a sight to behold." He comes up and wraps his arms around my waist from behind. "Two beautiful women in the kitchen."

Kelly throws a lime at him, but he ducks and it sails over his shoulder and plops onto the floor. "I'll show you a beautiful sight." She lifts up the knife, her eyes going wide and her smile turning lunatic large, and she cackles. We burst out laughing, Justin's chest vibrating against my back.

"Kell, I think you might just be an inch shy of crazy." I feel his lips next to my ear, and then his soft voice. "And, you, you just make me crazy."

I turn my head and press my lips to his, the kitchen forgotten for a moment, my insides flaring to life. He pulls away and swipes a finger across my bottom lip before nipping it gently one more time. "I've gotta go to the farm for a few hours, okay?"

I nod my head. "Okay." He releases me from his hold, places a parting kiss on my head, and leaves the kitchen with a goodbye to both me and Kelly.

"You are in so much trouble!" Kelly warns, collecting the bowl of lemons and limes and heading out to the bar.

I follow behind. "What? Why?" I push through the doors and help her load the fruit into the bar containers.

"You are so falling in love with him." She looks at me, a wicked grin on her face. "Admit it!"

"I am not!" I feel my face heat, and my heart begins to thump like a bass drum against my chest as I absorb her words, wondering if she's right.

"You are." She gives me a gentle shove. "Look at you right now. You're turning eight shades of red, and your mind is going a mile a minute! You love him!"

"Oh my God, Kelly." My hand moves absently to my mouth, covering the wide O shape it's now in, my wide eyes finding hers. "Shut the hell up."

She shrugs. "What's the big deal? He's fucking hot and obviously is completely into you, too."

"Noooo." My voice is low and quiet. "I can't fall in love with him. He's leaving in September."

"So?" She puts her hand on her hip and faces me. "Why can't you just go with him then? I mean, you haven't taken the job at the university yet, and there are bars and libraries in New York. You can get a job and just write there."

As if it was even possible, my heart thunders even more heavily as her words tumble through my brain. I look at her and shake my head. "Kell, we've only been dating a month. I can't even think about this right now."

She tilts her head and smirks. "You're gonna have to think about it sooner or later, 'cause you're falling, girl, and you're falling hard."

"Well, look what the cat dragged in," Jonathan calls out from the back of the barn as I hustle in. "Was beginning to wonder if we were going to see you at all this afternoon."

I pull on my work gloves and give him a snarl. "Shut it, brother. I told you I was having lunch with Syd and her dad this afternoon."

"Yeah, yeah. I just thought lunch ended three hours ago." He grabs a hay bale, cuts the twine, and spreads it across the stall he's in. "What the hell's going on with this girl, anyway?"

"What the fuck is that supposed to mean?" I grab my own bale and mirror his actions in the next stall over.

"This just isn't your style. Spending every night together, meeting the parents, showing up late to work."

"I like this girl, okay?" I huff out a tense breath and turn in his direction. "What's the big fucking deal?"

He stops what he's doing, walks over to the railing separating our stalls, and leans against it. "It's not a big deal, but you better remember that you're leaving come fall and I'd hate to see a girl screw that up for you."

I walk over and stand across from him, glad I have a couple inches on him because I don't like where this conversation is going. "Why the hell is this any of your damn business, anyway, Jonathan? Who I fuck or who I'm with has never been a concern of yours before."

His face reddens, a clear sign he's growing angrier. "Because, big brother, I've watched you work your ass off for the last two years to save the money to go make your dreams come true, and I'm the one that's going to be left behind here to cover your ass *and* your share of the work when you're gone. I don't want some girl screwing that up for you!"

Hearing his concern softens my temper. "She's not just some girl, Jonathan. I like her. I really like her. She's not like anyone else I've ever been with before."

He shakes his head, his lips forming a small frown before he looks at me. "So, what are you going to do? Are you in love with her?"

My blood freezes in my veins, a cold wave sweeping down my body at the mention of the 'L' word. I stare across the distance between us, not sure how to answer because I honestly don't know what I'm feeling. "Love? Shit, I don't know, man. How the hell am I supposed to know that?"

I turn my back to him, picking up the bale I deserted a moment ago, and use my nervous energy to break the hay apart and toss it around the stall. *Am I in love with her?* I mean, I like spending time with her. Definitely like spending the night with her. I have noticed that I'm starting to miss her presence, her smell, her laughter if I don't see her for a day. And, every time she walks into a room, my heart fucking feels like it's going to fall out of my damn chest.

"Well, you better figure it out, man. September's going to be here before you know it, and if you love her, it's going to make it damn hard to leave."

"Yeah, got it." I know he's looking out for me, but him stating the obvious just pisses me off. This isn't something I want to worry about right now. I like being with Sydney. I don't want to confuse this shit only a month in. We said that whatever happens, happens. No sense worrying about what might happen in three months.

We work the rest of the afternoon in silence, Jonathan more than aware that I'm in my head and giving me the space to deal with the thoughts I'm trying to pretend aren't racing through my mind. We finish up around six, and after a shower, I make myself a sandwich for dinner, eating alone at my small table.

She left me another love note a couple nights ago, and I keep reading the words over and over again, knowing for sure what I'm starting to feel but afraid to actually let myself feel it.

under a rain swept sky we kiss
wet lips fusing steam alight
flames flaring surprising miss
wolves threaten my dark night

I LEAVE THE TABLE AND MOVE TO THE COUCH, GRABBING MY guitar on the way. Her words still swirling in my head, I work out some chords to match the rhythm playing in my head. She's only written two small verses, but reading them has triggered a melody that I need to put down. I hum out the sounds floating in my mind and find the right notes, singing the words softly as I do. It's a process, but I keep moving over the notes again and again until I find the ones that feel good.

I look up at the clock and realize it's already after eight. *Shit!* I was so absorbed in what I was doing that I lost track of the time. I snap my guitar into the case, grab my keys, and head out the door to my truck.

Twenty minutes later, I walk into the bar, and the first thing I see is Sydney. As soon as her gaze finds me, her face softens and a beautiful smile breaks free as she lifts her hand to wave, mouthing a silent 'hi'.

My cheeks rise in return, and I stop in place, my heart doing the same as I realize, right now, right here, that fuck, I'm in love with this girl.

MICHELLE WINDSOR

CHAPTER TWELVE

I climb out of my truck and turn to help Syd slide out after me. It was a crazy night at the bar, and we're both exhausted. I follow her up the stairs to her apartment and then inside after she unlocks the door, grabbing the mail out of the box against the wall as I do. I throw the mail on the counter and toe off my boots, watching her do the same to hers.

"Are you hungry?" She walks to the fridge, opening it, and stares at the contents inside.

"Not really." I walk and stand behind her, looking to see if anything captures my eye. "I'm bone tired, though."

She spins around, her face inches from mine, and smiles coyly as she wraps her arms around my waist. "How tired?"

Even though I don't have to get up at the crack of dawn on Sundays, it's after two, and all I want to do is go to bed and sleep. "Tired." I give her a quick peck on the lips and pull out of her arms, a frown creasing her face as I push away and head to the bedroom. I hear her footsteps patter behind me.

"Justin, you okay?" I can hear the worry in her voice, and I get it. There hasn't been a single night spent together that we haven't ravished each other the minute we burst through the door. But I'm not going to lie. I'm freaking out a little about how quickly things have moved, comprehending that I've got it bad for this girl. I'm not quite sure what to do with all the feelings churning around in my head right now.

"Yeah, I'm good." I yank my shirt over my head, push my jeans off, then turn to face her. "I'm just completely wiped out. It's been a long day." I place a soft kiss on her lips and have to force myself to stop when the desire to pull her against me deepens. "Do you mind if we just go to sleep?"

Her eyes roam down my nearly naked body, her lip stuck between her teeth, her hunger evident, but she nods her head. "Um, sure, if you're tired." She turns and walks to the bathroom where I hear the water turn on as she washes her face.

Why the fuck am I fighting this? Every cell in my body wants to walk in there behind her, bend her over the sink, run my hands over inch of her body, and sink into her. I crave her, even when she's three feet away from me, and that scares the shit out of me. What the hell am I supposed to do now that I've realized I don't want to be without her? I'm leaving in a few months. This was the last damn thing I wanted or thought would happen. I get in the bed and lay back against the pillows, closing my eyes as I try to figure this shit out.

She slides in next to me and then curls herself around my body, my arms instinctively wrapping around her and pulling her closer. Her hand brushes gently back and forth over my bare chest to the cadence of her breathing until it finally slows and then stops, her body relaxed and sleeping. I lay there for over an hour, but I'm not able to do the same, so I finally ease myself out from under her and step quietly out of the room, shutting the door behind me.

I turn the light on in the open area of the living space, walk over to the fridge, and open it to grab a beer. I unlock the front door and stand out on the porch, sipping the beer as I listen to the sounds of the night. The leaves rustle softly in the light breeze wafting through the dark, and peepers are singing their night songs.

After a few minutes, I get chilly and move back inside to the couch.

I rustle through the books she has on the coffee table and pull out a tattered notebook I find in the pile. As I leaf through the book, I pause when I realize it's pages and pages of her writing. It seems to be mostly poems, thoughts, but also maybe the beginning of some stories. I skim through the pages and fix upon a poem she's written. She has "Choices" written at the top, and I wonder what inspired the words she wrote.

You can't make choices.
Won't you open up your mind?
It can get real hard sometimes,
Better when I'm sleeping all night,
When I'm up so late you're always on my mind,
Always on my mind.

But when there's nothing more,
You had the upper hand.
If this is it, I thought there'd be more.

Sitting in the chair, I can't find
The mask I need to disguise what's right.
Incapable of breathing, just fall down
One day we will all drown. It's fate evaporate.

But I think there's something more I could've said.
Deep in head, I fell asleep.

Circumstances lie. Why me?
Someone so unlucky to never see
Overall dramatic consequences.
Why can't we be mad at all people?

MICHELLE WINDSOR

> *It's not their fault,*
> *Unfairness reaching crosshairs.*
> *My little heart, in the apart, in the dark,*
> *Thinking.*
> *But soon I'll know*
> *I will see. It will come to me.*
> *Feel the breeze.*

I READ THE WORDS THREE TIMES AND SHAKE MY HEAD AT THEIR depth. This would make an amazing song. I walk over to the counter and grab my phone where I set it earlier, carrying it back to the couch. I open the camera app, hold it over the page, and snap a picture of the words. I flip through the pages until I reach the last one she's written on, and my heart soars when I read it.

> *In your arms*
> Justin, Justin, Justin… xo
>
> *cant tell if you're eyeing me, the irony it gets to me*
> *tape my mouth and lie to me i can't speak*
> *And i drink before you, calm down the nerves*
> *Why can't iI just be myself around you*
> *In your arms i feel safe*
> *But you try to keep me awake*
> *then iI go and sleep tight*
> *On my own he knows That i break*
> *And I know your struggles I'm alone in shackles*
> *Beating down the high beam park it here not the lobby*
> *Stop the shit you're stinking up the mix I'm making*
> *In the state of my mind, alaska, go ask ya*
> *In your arms i feel safe*

> *But you try to keep me awake*
> *then i go and sleep tight*
> *On my own he knows That*
> *i break away in his arms*
> *sometimes i don't feel safe*
> *he keeps me up so late*
> *but in your arms i stay safe*

It's dated three days ago. I read it one more time and know it won't be enough so I take a picture of this page, too. She's insanely talented. I didn't realize until seeing her thoughts, her words written down. There is still so much for me to learn about her. I sit for another half hour reading her words and know I'm not going to sleep tonight.

I tip-toe back into the bedroom, pausing to watch her as she sleeps, her hair scattered in a thousand directions around her head, her breath whispering out between her puffy lips, and my heart surges. Yes, I'm in love with her. There's not a doubt anymore as I look at her, and this time, I'm only filled with a sense of peace, not fear. I pluck my jeans and shirt off the floor and then quietly backtrack to the living area again to put them on, followed by my boots. I rip a piece of paper from the notebook and jot down a few words.

> Syd,
> Couldn't sleep so went home.
> Come on out to the farm later if you want.
> Love,
> Justin

MICHELLE WINDSOR

CHAPTER THIRTEEN

I stretch and roll over, yawning as I do, sulking when I realize Justin isn't in the bed with me. I glance at the alarm clock, noting that it's after nine and know he's used to getting up much earlier than that. I slip out of bed, use the bathroom, and sneak into the kitchen to surprise him, but find out the surprise is on me when all I discover is a note left on the counter.

I read it and stare at the last two lines of the note: Love, Justin. He wrote love. We haven't said that word to each other yet. Not that I haven't wondered about it since Kelly brought it up yesterday, but now, here it is on paper. I'm not going to read too much into it. It's just a little word that lots of people use when signing a note or letter. Okay, maybe not a little word.

I hold the note to my chest and spin around in a happy circle, allowing myself one small celebration over the note, and then pull myself together. I make coffee and can't stop smiling as I hum "Crazy" while I scoop coffee into the filter. Justin and I danced to that last night during our traditional after hours 'rhythm' lesson, him crooning every word softly as we swayed.

Is this what love feels like? I like it if it is. I wait for the coffee to brew and sort through the mail Justin tossed on the counter last night, freezing when I see the return address on one of the envelopes. *Holy crap!* It's from one of the biggest publishing companies in the States! My hands shake as I snag it from the pile and rip open the seal. I pull out the letter, the very thick letter I might add, and unfold it.

DEAR MS. PORTER,

We are extremely delighted that you and your agent chose to submit your work to our house and would be thrilled if you would consider publishing with us. We absolutely loved your book and can't believe it's a debut novel. The writing is outstanding, and we feel strongly that this story will resonate with many readers and move quickly onto the best seller list. To show our commitment and belief in you, please find enclosed a contract for your review.

My eyes scan the rest of the letter and the contract before I drop it on the counter and scream. "Oh my God! They want me!"

Coffee forgotten, I run to my room, throw on the first thing I grab from my closet, slide my feet into a pair of sandals, and grab my keys and the letter as I race from the house. Fifteen minutes later, I pull up in front of Justin's cottage, throw the car in park, and run inside.

I look around and see he's not here so head back out and over to the barn. I walk into the dark, cool space and call out his name. "Justin?"

"Yo!" His head pops out from the loft above, a grin on his sweaty face. "You came!"

I smile back and move to the ladder, clenching the letter between my teeth so I can use my hands to climb up. I look as I move up the rungs and see him at the top waiting for me, hand stretched out to help me with the final couple steps.

"Whatcha got there?" He yanks the letter out of my mouth just as I begin hopping up and down.

"I got it! They want to publish my book, Justin!" I point to the letter as he's trying to read it, still hopping in place. "They are like *the* biggest publication house! Can you believe it?" I shriek as I watch him finish scanning the letter, his smile growing in size as he does.

"Syd! This is amazing!" He picks me up and spins me around, slamming a kiss down on my mouth when he comes to a stop. "I'm so proud of you! Congratulations!"

I pick the letter up where it dropped when he spun me around and point to one of the paragraphs. "They want to give me a thirty-thousand-dollar advance!" I look up at him with wide eyes. "Thirty-thousand, Justin!"

"Looks like you're buying dinner tonight!" He plants another kiss on my lips, but this time, when the letter drifts to the ground, it's because it slips from my fingers as I wrap my arms around him and tangle them in his hair. Our kiss grows more heated, his hands slipping under the skirt of my sundress to grasp onto my ass as he pushes his groin into me.

I tear my lips away from his and lock my gaze on him, my blood surging through my veins when I see the heat in them. I place my hand flat against his chest and push, stepping forward as I do until he falls back into a sitting position on a stack of hay bales. I kick my sandals off and move to straddle him, but not before I slide my panties down and off, my eyes never leaving his, my grin naughty as his widens in surprise.

"Are you still tired?" I ask huskily as I seat myself across his legs and rock my naked core against his hard length.

"Not even a little." His hand is on the back of my head, bringing it forward as he slams his lips to mine, his tongue sweeping across, forcing them apart, then delving inside. I moan when his other hand travels to my breast and squeezes gently, his lips now grazing a trail down my neck. He pushes the strap of my dress down until my breast is free, seals his lips over my nipple, and sucks hard. My head falls back and I arch into him, feeling my peak tighten and grow taut under his tongue.

"That feels so good, Justin." I rock my pelvis into his length again, his lips flipping a switch that has my core throbbing. I grip the back of his neck and use it as leverage to lift myself up, then slowly slide my clit against the hard denim covering his cock to try to find some relief.

Justin finally seems to get the message and tears his mouth away from my breast. He moves to unbutton his jeans and then wiggles to lower them until his cock springs free. I groan and wrap my hand around it, sliding it up and down the silk of his length, my core dripping now.

He's nipping at my neck and gripping my waist and then lifting me so I'm over him. "Jesus Christ, get the fuck on me, Sydney. I want to feel you around me." His words come out in pants, and I move to line his cock up underneath me, and then slowly lower myself on top of him.

I bite my lip as his crown slips past my center, and then I push all the way down, groaning when I'm fully seated. His mouth finds mine and crushes against it, his hips moving to thrust up, surging into mine. I press my knees down into the hay and slide myself up and down his hard shaft, my clit rubbing against his coarse hair, stimulating me every time I grind myself home.

We're both panting and clinging to each other, trying to keep our lips fused as we rock together, our tempo increasing as we build toward our climax. I feel myself begin to fly higher, my body tingling, and I know I'm close.

"I'm going to come." I grip his back, digging my short nails into his skin as I grind myself harder, my mouth at his ear, my breaths coming out in short bursts.

"Me too! Come with me, Syd. Come with me." He squeezes me tight in his arms, thrusting hard and deep one more time, my pussy clenching around him like a vise as he does, then pulsing wildly as I feel his warm seed explode inside of me.

"Oh my God, oh my God, oh my God," tumbles from my mouth as I cling to him, my body shuddering against his as aftershocks shiver through me. His lips are kissing my neck and then moving across my cheek until they find my mouth. He drops soft kisses against them, his breaths ragged, his forehead resting against mine. My eyes flutter open to find his looking at me intensely. He drops another soft kiss, not breaking my gaze, and then whispers, "I love you," before kissing me softly again.

I move to pull back, but his grip on me tightens and he shakes his head. "Don't move." He kisses me again. "Just stay like this for another minute. You don't have to say it back. But I want to remember this feeling, the way you feel on top of me, around me. I don't ever want to forget it."

My heart flares, and I swear it feels like it's on fire. I clench my fingers around the nape of his neck and kiss him. I kiss him with every ounce of emotion I am feeling, my body pressed up against his until I feel like we are one, my breath becoming his breath. When I finally tear away from him, it's only because I need to speak. It comes out softly. "I love you, too Justin."

We hold each other for a long time before we finally break apart, me lifting myself off of him. He pulls a handkerchief out of his back pocket and gently helps me clean myself up before I slide my panties back on. He pulls his jeans up, rises, and pulls me into his arms.

"Is this too soon? It's only been a little over a month." His chest vibrates as he asks out loud what we both may be thinking.

I shrug in his arms. "I don't know. How long does love take?" I turn my gaze up to his. "I just know this feels good. It feels right, definitely different than anything else."

He leans down and sweeps several kisses over my lips before speaking. "I don't know how long love takes. I guess one month." He smiles and places a kiss on the tip of my nose. "And this feels so much more than good. It feels fucking amazing."

I giggle and push myself gently out of his arms, nodding as I do. "You are pretty amazing, Justin Jeffries; I'll give you that."

He catches my hand and pulls me back toward him. "You're

going to be a published author. That's pretty damn amazing, too." He slides his hand to my cheek, pulls my face to his, and kisses me tenderly. "Seriously, congratulations. I know it's what you really wanted. I'm so happy for you."

"Thank you. That means a lot." I kiss him one more time and shrug. "What now?"

"Let's go tell everyone the good news! We need to celebrate." He moves down the ladder first and then helps me as I descend after him.

We walk back to the cottage, hand in hand, talking about who we should go tell first. "Do you mind if I take a shower first? I drove right over here after opening the letter and didn't even brush my teeth!"

"Can I wash your back?" I look over to see him grinning like a bandit.

I laugh loudly and nod my head in agreement. "Sounds like the perfect way to start our celebration."

He pulls me into his arms and raises his brows mockingly. "You mean, continue the celebration?"

I blush and wrap my arms around him, the sun warming my face as I look up at him. "Have I told you that I love you?"

He looks down and frowns. "You do?"

"I do."

"Good, 'cause I love you, too."

CHAPTER FOURTEEN

It's been six glorious weeks since Justin and I declared our love for each other, and our feelings and time spent together have only grown. I glance at the calendar; it's August fourth. Less than a month until Justin heads to New York City. Although neither of us has brought it up, I know the fact that he's leaving soon is on both of our minds.

I've signed the contract with the publishing house, and we've begun work on cover designs and edits for the book. I also let the university know I won't be taking the position they offered. I think they were disappointed but also elated to hear my publishing news. After all, if by some miracle I do hit the best-seller list, they will be able to tout me as a success story.

How can everything be so absolutely perfect, yet all I feel in the pit of my stomach is fear? I'm so afraid of what's going to happen to me and Justin in another four weeks, and if the book will do well, and I just can't help but wonder what all of it means for my life overall. That doesn't even begin to cover the madness that's now swirling around all the events for Kelly's wedding.

Her wedding is the first Saturday in October, so the next six weeks will be filled with dress fittings, flower appointments, bridal showers, and of course, her bachelorette party. So much to do! But today, today I'm not going to think about any of it. It's Sunday and I have the day off. Unfortunately, Justin doesn't. His family is out haying the fields today. The next six days are supposed to be hot, clear, and sunny, and apparently, that's what they need to ensure the hay can dry once it's cut, and then they'll bale it. Who knew I'd become a hay bale expert over the summer?

For the last several weeks, the temperatures have been soaring into the hundreds, so I'm making some cold salads, sandwiches, and a big jug of ice cold lemonade to take to the boys for lunch. Everything is ready except for me, so I scramble to the bathroom to take a quick shower and get dressed.

A short while later, I pull into the farm and notice all the vehicles are parked in the driveway. I expected them to all be out in the fields, so a sense of alarm triggers my pulse, it's rhythm picking up as I wonder what could be wrong. I park next to Justin's truck and, instead of grabbing the food I've prepared, I shut the door and head straight for the main house. I raise my hand to knock on the door, but it swings open before I can. Justin is standing in the doorway, a smile lifting his face.

"Hey, beautiful." He pulls me into his arms and presses his very hot lips to mine.

I pull away and place my hand on his forehead. "You're burning up!"

"Come in." He pulls me inside and shuts the door behind me. "It's a Goddamn furnace out there today. We all had to come in for a while or risk getting heat stroke."

"So, everyone's okay?" My heart slows to its normal cadence as relief sweeps through me.

He tilts his head and pushes his ball cap off his head as he runs his fingers through his sweaty hair, a lopsided grin on his face. "Syd, were you worried about us?"

"Of course, I was worried about you guys!" I brush past him

and move toward the kitchen, where I'm sure the rest of the family will be. "I was expecting you to all be in the fields."

I hear him clomp up behind me in his work boots, feel his grip on my waist, and then he's hauling my back up against his front. "Have I told you lately that I love you?"

His breath tickles my ear as he murmurs, but that isn't the reason I'm smiling. "No, not lately," I whisper back.

"I do." He kisses my neck, the heat of his lips scorching my skin delightfully.

"You do?" I drag my lower lip between my teeth.

"So fucking much, babe." He nuzzles his face into my neck as his grip around me tightens.

"Good, 'cause I love you, too." I wrap my hands around his and squeeze. "So much." I'm glad he's holding on so tightly to me because, I swear, I feel so light I could practically float away right now. I start moving again, his grip loosening as I do, but his hand stays on my waist as he follows next to me.

I push open the kitchen door and wave at his family around the table. They all look red, sweaty, and exhausted. "Hey, guys. ya'll okay?"

They all nod in unison and return my greeting. Mrs. Jeffries, or Pam, as she insists I call her, moves to get up from the table, but I motion for her to stay. "Have you guys eaten?"

They shake their heads again, in unison, before Pam speaks. "I was just going to finish this glass of water and put something together for everyone."

I beam, knowing my lunch is going to be a saving grace for them today. "Ya'll sit right there and relax. I made up some lunch that I was going to bring out to the fields, so let me go get it out of the car." I turn to Justin, whose expression is nothing short of adoration. "Can you come help me?"

"Uh, yeah. Of course." He turns to the table. "Be right back."

Five minutes later, we're setting the Tupperware bowls of potato and macaroni salad on the table, followed by the tray of sandwiches I made. Jonathan takes the large thermos of lemonade I'm holding and places it on the counter but not before dropping a kiss on my forehead. "You're the best."

We sit and eat, their coloring finally toning down to a light pink, the cool air of the house and the food a relaxing comfort to them all. Everyone's silent throughout the meal, but it's not an uncomfortable silence, quite the opposite in fact. There's an unspoken comfort between all of us as we share this Sunday meal, a real sense of family and love present around the table.

"Sydney, I can't thank you enough for bringing this today. You're a dream come true." Pam reaches over and pats my hand, her soft eyes meeting mine in thanks.

"I'm so happy I could do something to help. I know it's hot as Hades out there."

"Thank goodness that even in hell, people get an occasional sip of water." He gives me a sly grin as I register he's throwing the very words I tossed at him the day we met in the bar.

I laugh out loud before responding. "Touché."

Everyone else around the table is looking at us like we've gone a little mad, so Justin explains. "It's an inside joke, a quote she teased me with once upon a time."

They all nod like they understand, but the look in their eyes makes it all too clear that they still think we're a bit bonkers. And it's okay. Maybe we are. But I'll take feeling bonkers anytime if it means feeling like this.

Pam and I work to clear the table and clean up the dishes, while the boys sit at the table and discuss the rest of the cutting that needs to be done. It's decided they'll break until after five this evening, in hopes it will be a little cooler but before the dew sets on the hay. Jonathan declares he's going to take a nap, at which Mr. Jeffries, Tom, exclaims the same. Pam says she's going to catch up on some DVR shows and leaves me and Justin alone in the kitchen.

"So, what do you want to do, farm boy?" I grin mischievously at him, my intent all too clear.

"I have an idea." He looks me up and down and then nods his head. "Guess you're dressed okay."

I look down at the cut-off jean shorts, white tank top, and chucks I'm wearing and then back up at him. "Dressed okay for what?"

He grabs my hand and pulls me toward the back-kitchen door. "Come on, I'll show you."

I LEAD HER TO THE LARGE SHED-LIKE GARAGE THAT'S NEAR THE BARN and enter the code for the lock on the door. I pull it open when I get the green light and flick the switch on the wall, illuminating the large space. We store the tractors, mowers, and other equipment in here, but what I head for are the three ATVs on the far side of the space.

"You ever been on one of these before?" I point to the four-wheeled, motorcycle-like vehicles and grin.

"Actually, believe it or not, I have." I turn to her and raise my brows in surprise as she shrugs. "Old boyfriend used to be crazy about them."

I grimace, not wanting to hear or admit there's ever been anyone in her life before me. "Wanna take a ride with me? There's someplace I want to take you."

"Sure!" She walks over and hops onto the closest one, straddling the seat, a huge smile on her face. "Let's go!"

"Slow down there, Evil Knievel!" I walk to the wall, grab a couple helmets hanging on hooks, and hand one to her.

"Ugh!" She looks at it and frowns. "Do I have to? It's so damn hot out and this is going to make it worse."

"Well, if we crash and you crack that pretty head of yours, that would be even worse." I pull the helmet out of her hands and place it overhead, fastening and tightening the strap under her chin to hold it firmly in place. I brush a kiss against her lips and then pull a helmet on my own head. "You look gorgeous, even as a helmet head."

She sticks her tongue out at me as I swing my leg over the bike and seat myself in front of her. I click on the engine, push the button to start it, gunning the gas as I do, and rev the engine a bit to scare her. It works because her arms snake around my middle and grab on firmly.

I maneuver the ATV out the shed door and then zoom off across the yard, up through the fields, and up into the woods. I cruise easily on the beaten path for about twenty-five minutes, climbing steadily upwards, the breeze from the ride and shade from the trees keeping us relatively cool. When we come to a clearing, I cut the engine, remove my helmet, and then jump off to help her do the same.

Her eyes scanning the area, a look of wonder dancing across her features, and I smile. "Justin, this place is beautiful!"

I look around at the small clearing and nod. It's located almost at the top of the largest hill on our property, and a hidden gem if I ever saw one. There's a small brook that runs through one side of the grass and flower-covered field, but the real treasure is the small pond that sits right in the middle. It's stream fed and crystal clear, its temperature always cold and refreshing. I come up here a lot when I need to think or clear my head and tell her just that.

She reaches down, unties her laces, and kicks her sneakers off beside the ATV. I watch as she squishes her toes in the mossy grass and then looks up at me, a delighted smile lifting her cheeks. "It's so soft."

"Want to go for a swim?" I point to the pond and pull my shirt over my head, making it clear that I'm going in no matter what her reply, and then start unbuttoning my jeans.

"But I don't have a suit?" She frowns, a look of disappointment clouding her features. "Why didn't you tell me to bring one?" She crosses her arms, her eyes watching me as I drop my pants, then my boxers, and grin when I see them shift wide in surprise as she realizes what's happening.

I waggle my brows and smirk when her mouth opens wide. "Suit optional up here, baby." Then, I run and leap into the pond, the cold water wrapping around my body in welcome relief as I sink down and then push myself back to the surface.

I'm not really surprised when I sweep my gaze in a circle to see Sydney stripping off her clothes in quick fashion, a wicked gleam in her eye as she smiles at me. "You don't have to ask me twice."

I watch as she dashes across the short distance to the pond and then yells when she forms a cannonball and jumps right toward me. The water splashes up and over me as she submerges below the surface, drenching me all over again. It's so unbelievably refreshing after the morning spent in the heat that I revel in its cool comfort.

She bursts up beside me, water sliding down her long hair, a look of complete joy on her face. She catches her breath and swims to me, wrapping her arms around my neck and her legs around my waist. "How come you haven't brought me here before? I love it."

I watch the water drip off her nose and lashes and dart my tongue out, running it across her lips to capture the cool taste of the liquid lining them. She kisses me, thrusting herself closer, and I feel myself harden under her. I break away from the kiss and swirl us around in the water, fascinated when she leans back, her hair rippling out and around her like a halo. Her hard nipples are peeking just above the surface, her hands floating freely beside her, and I swear I have never seen anything more Goddamn beautiful in my life.

When I pull her back to me, I place my hand on her lower back, lifting her flush against my body, and gaze into her eyes. "Move to New York with me."

Her brows rise in reaction to how wide her eyes just popped, and I wonder for a brief moment who's more surprised by my statement. I've been thinking about asking her for the last week or so but didn't actually plan to act on it yet.

"You want me to move to New York with you?" She echoes my request, my demand, I think checking that she really heard me correctly.

I nod my head as I rest it against hers. "I don't want this to end. I can't imagine my days without you in them now."

Her lip is clenched between her grinding teeth, her brows furrowed as she wraps her arms more tightly around my neck and hugs herself to me. Her words are muffled when she finally responds. "I don't know, Justin. It's so scary. We've only known each other a few months. What if it doesn't work?"

I grip her a little harder, my legs still kicking to keep us afloat, and crush her even closer to me. "How can this not work? Look at us. I love you. I love you so damn much, when I think of being without you, my fucking heart aches."

She pushes herself back so she's looking into my eyes, tears, not water anymore, sliding in slow tendrils down her cheeks. "I love you, too, Justin. So much." Her lips find mine and devour them as if she hasn't eaten in days. My cock grows hard as she grinds herself against me in the depths of the water, so I move as gracefully as I can to the shore and carry her out and onto the grass.

We speak no words. The only sounds are our moans drifting in the breeze with each thrust and push of our bodies as we worship each other. After, we lay spent, entwined, our naked skin cool against the soft grass, her fingers caressing the hairs on my arm as they run back and forth.

"I can't leave until after Kelly's wedding, okay?" Her question is tentative, but I know she's made her decision and my heart feels like it's going to leap out of my chest.

I untangle myself from her and move to loom over her instead. "You'll come?" I can't hide the excitement and relief in the tone of my voice and I don't care.

She nods her head and gives me the sweetest smile, one I read as blissful surrender to a love neither of us wants to fight.

CHAPTER FIFTEEN

The last month has flown by in a whirlwind of time with Justin, with Kelly, and with my dad. We've told everyone I'm going to move to New York after the wedding, and although we don't think anyone was too surprised, Kelly definitely isn't happy. I recall our conversation right after I told her.

"You're really going to leave? Just like that? After only dating him a few months?" Her face is pinched in anger as she drums her fingers against the beer bottle in her grip. We just finished our Friday night shift, and I finally worked up the nerve to tell her.

"I love him, Kelly. We want to be together." I reach out my hand and cover her fingers to stop their incessant tapping. "I'm not leaving 'til after the wedding, though. I'm going to be here for you every moment up until then."

"And what about after, huh?" She takes a long draw of the beer and then slams the bottle back to the table. "What about when Adam and I have our first big married fight, or when I get pregnant? And, Syd, who's going to sing "Crazy" with me after our shifts?"

Her voice is whiny now, and I know deep down she's really happy for me but just needs these few moments to feel sorry for herself. "You can call me anytime, day or night, and you know I'll answer. When you get pregnant, you can bet your ass I'll be there in the delivery room with you, no matter what. And, well, just Facetime me and I'll sing "Crazy" with you any ole time you want."

She continues to sulk for a few more minutes until the corners of her mouth finally lift, forming the smallest of smiles. "'Cause you know Adam can't stand the sight of blood, right? You have to be in the delivery room with me, Syd."

I laugh and relief washes over me when I know she's going to eventually be okay with my leaving. "I won't miss a single baby you deliver."

I look over at my best friend and smile. Tonight's the last time that Justin is performing. He's leaving on Monday. The crowd is the biggest I've ever seen at Hook's, with people lined up down the street waiting for someone to leave so another can enter. Justin's already halfway through his second set, and I just want the night to end so I can have him all to myself.

Once he leaves, I won't get to see him again until Kelly's wedding. That's a whole month. I already miss him and he's not even gone yet. He catches me watching him across the bar and gives me a smile as his voice continues to float through the room, mesmerizing everyone but especially me. A long sigh leaves my body as I try to push away the thought of being without him for a month and get back to work.

KELLY PUSHES THE DOOR CLOSED TIGHTLY AND FLIPS THE LOCK after pushing the last few stragglers out of the bar. It's after one in the morning, and we're feeling a little anxious knowing this is Justin's last night. "Thank fucking hallelujah! I thought they were never going to leave!"

"Amen, sister!" I call out in agreement and then pull our standard five dollars out of the tip jar and slap it on the bar. I look at Kelly and grin as she walks up and swipes it off the counter.

She surprises me when she stops in front of Justin and thrusts the money out to him. "I think you should do the honors, Justin, since it's your last night and all."

My heart swells a little, thinking it may actually be the nicest thing Kelly's done or said to Justin since we've been dating. He looks at her, uncertainty in his expression, as he slides the money out from her fingers. "You sure? This is your and Syd's thing."

"Yeah, I'm sure." She walks away quickly, which I know is her way of avoiding any further emotion over the issue. "Consider it my goodbye gift to you."

"Gee, thanks, Kell." His tone is a little sarcastic, but when he looks at me and pops his eyes wide in a 'holy hell' kind of look, I know he really is thankful. He walks over to the jukebox, and while he's making his selections, Kelly and I start the nightly clean-up. We both freeze and look at each other, then at him, when the first notes of the song he plays come blaring over the speakers.

He shrugs and gives us an aloof smile. "You didn't think I was going to spend my last night without one more rendition of "Crazy" by you two, did you?"

Kelly and I screech, yelling how much we love him, and then scramble to the dance floor for our weekly ritual of butchering Patsy Cline, as Justin looks on and laughs. *I really, really love that man.*

When the song ends, Kell and I get back to cleaning up the bar, and Justin packs up his gear, and when we're done, we all finally sit at one of the tables and have a drink together. We talk about the fun we've had each weekend, which fan might be Justin's craziest, and laugh at all the things we'll miss about working together.

About twenty minutes in, the familiar sounds of "Linger" come over the speakers, and Justin's gaze sweeps and locks on mine.

Kelly rises from the table, makes an excuse about going to start the dishwasher, and exits the room quickly. We both stand and move in tandem over to the dance floor, his arms enveloping me in a tight embrace before we slowly sway to the music.

"What am I going to do without you in my arms for the next month?" His voice is a whisper in my ear as he pulls me even closer.

I just shake my head, my voice lost as I fight the tears forming in my eyes. I know this isn't forever. Four weeks really isn't a long time. But, we've spent every night of the last four months together, so I know not having his chest to fall against each night is going to be an adjustment. His hand slithers between us and under my chin to lift my face, his lips sealing over mine in a sweet kiss. I savor the kiss, wanting to burn it to memory; the way his lips are always so warm, so soft, and leave mine tingling as we pull apart.

His lips move to my ear. "Have I told you lately that I love you?"

I'm still not able to find my voice so I simply shake my head no.

"I do."

I shake my head again, the tears now falling freely from my eyes. He stops moving and cradles my face in his hands, kissing away the salty trails and then my closed eyelids.

"I love you so much, Syd. We'll be together again before you know it."

When I finally open my eyes and nod my head, my words come out hoarse. "I love you, too. So much. I'm already counting the days."

Brooklyn is kind of amazing. I never thought in a million years I would feel so at home in a place that doesn't have a single cow or barn in a thirty-mile radius. My friend Andrea set me up with a loft apartment in the Bushwick neighborhood for the bargain price of twenty-five hundred bucks a month. It's pretty small, but when Sydney comes, we'll look for a bigger place to settle into.

Not having Sydney here with me is the only thing that makes this move hard. We've spoken every day on the phone, usually several times a day, actually, and I think we've given new meaning to burning up the phone lines during our nightly Facetime chats. But we're ten days in and only have twenty-three to go until Kelly's wedding.

I'm going to fly back for the wedding, and then we'll both drive back out in Syd's car. I didn't bring my truck, knowing I could get around anywhere with the subway, but she's adamant about having her own vehicle. She might change her mind once she discovers how much parking is around here, but I'll let her figure that out on her own.

Right now, I'm headed to the studio to work out a few more tracks with Andrea. We've only laid down two so far, but I think it's going pretty well. He likes what I have but wants me to try to dig down a little and see if I can't come up with a few deeper songs. Acoustic songs, like "Perfect" and "Let Her Go" are all the rage right now. Not having Sydney in my arms every night is definitely giving me good material to write about, so I feel good about hammering out some new stuff for him.

The square, two-story building comes into view, and I stop in front of the black door with simple, white lettering stating

Rambling Recording, the only thing indicating anything musical about the place. After ringing the buzzer, I wait for the lock to release and then make my way inside. Andrea's sitting behind the large mixing board listening to someone else play right now, so settle in one of the small music rooms.

I take out my guitar and, with Sydney on my mind, start playing some of the chords I put together for one of her poems. I want to surprise her and play it at Kelly's wedding. I'm not sure how long I've actually been in the room and am startled when Andrea claps his hands as I croon out the last notes of the song for Syd.

"Man, that song is amazing! Exactly what I wanted to hear from you!" He claps me on the back and sits across from me. "Play it again. I want to hear it from the beginning."

I stare at him for a minute, not sure how to explain that it's not my song, not my words, and that it's for someone else, but his enthusiasm gets in the way, and the reason I'm playing the song gets buried in his insistence at its quality. "Come on, man, no over-thinking here; just play it. It's good, I'm telling you straight up!"

My fingers seem to have a mind of their own as they strum the melody to the song again, my voice singing her words, the sound drowning out all common sense. When I'm done, he yells loudly, pumps his fist in the air, and jumps around in a circle. "That's going to be a hit, man! I can feel it in my bones!"

I smile and nod my head earnestly, the praise a feeling I need and seem to crave since I've started working with him. "Thanks, A."

"Tell me you've got some more like that!" He sits on the stool beside me, his knee bouncing wildly as he taps his foot non-stop against the floor. His energy is palpable and contagious, feeding and heightening the drive already pumping through my veins.

"I've got something else." I flip through the pages of my notebook and play the cords I recently put together for the "Choices" poem that Syd wrote. I mean, I know these are her words, but it's my music, and it's my music that makes them a song, so what I'm doing doesn't feel entirely wrong. As I watch A's face light up, any feelings of guilt wash away in his excitement and encouragement.

Later that night, I'm home alone in the loft, missing every single thing about Sydney, and smile when I see her number come up on my phone. "Hey, babe. I was just thinking about you. I'm missing you hard tonight."

"Hey. I miss you, too. So much. The days at the library seem so long now that I know I'm not coming home to you."

"Not too much longer, though. Only twenty-three more days." I walk over to the calendar I have on the wall and mark another X in the countdown to Kelly's wedding.

"I know, and next week is my last at the library. I'll be crazy busy helping Kell with all the wedding stuff after that, so it should go by fast."

"Everything all set for the bachelorette party this weekend?" I ask, not really wanting to know all the details, but still wanting to be supportive.

"Ugh, yes. She's driving me crazy with all her silly rules, though." She lets out a long sigh. "I'll be happy when it's over. Anyway, how was your day? Did you work on anything new with Andrea?"

"It was really good actually. He heard a couple new songs and really liked them, so we're going to work on recording them over the next couple days."

"That's awesome, babe!" I hear her clap her hands in happiness and my heart contracts painfully, reminding me that I'm not telling her the whole truth. I pretend to myself that it's because I still want to surprise her at the wedding, but deep down, I know I should tell her right now that the songs are actually hers. "When can I hear them?"

"Soon, baby, soon." My answer says more to me than it does to her, but I swallow and try to tamp down the guilt I feel, wanting success it seems at any cost.

LOVE NOTES

CHAPTER SIXTEEN

I walk out of the arrivals terminal at JFK airport and almost giggle with glee when I see a man in a dark suit holding a sign with my name on it. If this doesn't make me feel like I've arrived, I'm not sure what does. I walk up to him, a wide grin that is impossible to wipe off my face, stretching my cheeks. "I'm Ms. Porter." I point to myself in case it's not clear. "Sydney Porter."

His brows rise sardonically as he lowers the sign and his gaze does a quick sweep down my attire. I'm wearing one of my standard librarian work outfits, thinking it was appropriate for a book meeting. The publisher called yesterday and asked if I'd be available to fly in for a meeting with them to discuss numerous things about the book. I was able to get my library hours covered easily enough, and Kelly's party isn't until Friday, so here I am.

It was so hard not to tell Justin last night that I'd be coming today, but I really want to surprise him. I'm only meeting with the publication house this afternoon, so I have all of tonight and tomorrow to spend with him. My heart flutters and my insides turn to mush when I think about seeing him again. Only a few more hours.

"Do you have any baggage, Ms. Porter?" He looks in the direction of the baggage claim area and back at me.

"Oh no." I pull at the small carry-on I have with me. "It's just this. Only a quick trip, you see."

He nods, brows rising again, and moves to take the bag from me. "Yes, I see."

I release my hold on the bag and then follow behind him as he rolls it out of the airport and to a waiting town car. He helps me into the back seat and then loads the luggage into the trunk. Once he's settled in the driver's seat, he pulls out into traffic. "Ms. Porter, is there a hotel you're checking in to, or am I bringing you straight to the publishing house?"

"Oh, I'm staying in Brooklyn with my boyfriend while I'm here. I'm surprising him." I'm babbling, and I know it, but I'm full of nervous energy and can't seem to stop myself. "So, you can just take me to the office."

"Lovely. Thank you." His tone is dry and offers not one bit of comfort. I want so badly to phone Justin and tell him about the meeting and that I'm here, but that would ruin the surprise. Instead, I sit and squirm in my seat for just a bit longer.

Five long hours later, I gather all my notes from the meetings, find my luggage, and make my way out of the building. The meetings were amazing, and I can't wait to tell Justin all about them. I walk to the sidewalk and throw my hand out, trying to pretend I've hailed a cab a thousand times. I've actually watched pretty much every episode of "Sex and the City" and hope I'm channeling Carrie Bradshaw effectively.

I'm delighted when a cab comes to a halt next to me, and clap my hands at my success. *I can do this New York City stuff!* I open the door and slide into the seat, pulling my bag in beside me as I slam the door shut. "Rambling Recording Studio in Brooklyn, please."

"Jesus Christ, lady. You're going to fucking Brooklyn? Just my luck. You know how much that's gonna cost ya? Maybe you should just take the subway." His bloodshot eyes are staring angrily at me from the rearview as he waits for me to respond.

"I've got the fare, and I prefer a taxi. Let's go." I state, pretending to be much braver than I really feel.

"How 'bout a real address then, babe. You don't seriously think I'm going to know where some studio in Brooklyn is, do ya?" He's already pulling into traffic, so I feel like I've won a small victory, even if I screwed up with the address. I pull it up quickly on my phone and rattle it off to him.

"Damn yuppies. Too good for the subway," he responds, muttering some more about what a pain in the ass it is going to Brooklyn at four in the afternoon on a weekday and how I better give him a good tip. I drown him out as I take in the city sights, my stomach somersaulting with nerves as we get closer and closer.

He finally pulls up in front of a short, square building, announcing we're here. I look and, sure enough, see the lettering on the door for Rambling Recording. "It's fifty-three bucks, lady."

I pull three twenties from my wallet, shove them in the pocket in the plexiglass separating us, and tell him to keep the change. I get out of the car, pulling my suitcase behind me, and reach for the handle, frowning when it doesn't turn. I take out my phone and look at the time. It's a little before five, but Justin told me he's usually at the studio until seven or eight most nights.

I jump when a voice crackles out at me from a box near the door. "Who ya looking for?"

I lean over and speak loudly into the box. "I'm here to see Justin Jeffries."

"You don't have to yell." I hear a loud switch on the lock of the door and swing my gaze to it. "Pull the door open, sweetie."

Oh my God, I must look like a complete moron. I grip the handle, pull, and nod like a dummy when the door swings open. It takes a moment for my eyes to adjust to the dark hallway once the door slams behind me, but when they do, I walk forward toward a

LOVE NOTES

light I see at the end of the hall. As I get closer, I recognize Justin's voice, and I pick up speed, not wanting to wait another minute to see him.

The light is spilling out from a large window, illuminating two men sitting behind a huge board filled with enough switches and toggles to make anyone's mind spin. And beyond them, behind another glass wall, Justin sits on a stool, playing his guitar, singing into a mic.

I leave my luggage outside the room and then quietly open the door and step into the room with the two men. I'm assuming one of them must be Andrea. They don't hear me enter, so I just stand and listen, my head tilted as I do. Something sounds familiar, but I don't recognize the music, so I know this must be one of his new songs. His eyes are closed as he sings, so he still hasn't seen me, which gives me more time to listen.

Stop the shit
you're stinking up the mix I'm making
In the state of my mind
alaska go ask her
In your arms I feel safe
But you try to keep me awake
then I go and sleep tight

I TAKE IN A SHARP BREATH AND HOLD IT AS THE LYRICS HE JUST sang hit home. *Alaska, go ask her? These are my words.* I remember writing this poem and trying to think of a faraway place a person might go to collect their state of mind. How the hell did he get my poem? I scoff in anger and then cover my mouth as the two men turn around, finally realizing I'm in the room. One of them stands and turns to me. "Oh, hey, sorry. Didn't see you there. Can I help you?"

My eyes fly from the man and through the glass to Justin, who has stopped singing and is staring out at me, a look of surprised joy on his face. I point to the window and then shake my finger no as I back out of the room. I watch as his face changes from joy to fear, and then turn and flee from the building.

MY HEART STOPS IN MY CHEST WHEN I OPEN MY EYES AND SEE Sydney standing in the room with Andrea and Mike. Joy zings through my body. She's here! I move to put the guitar down, but then freeze when I actually notice the expression on her face and then see her wave her finger no in dismissal at me. Every ounce of joy immediately thickens to heavy fear as I watch her turn and run out of the room.

I bolt from the room, slamming the door into the wall as I do, and run down the hall after her, Andrea yelling behind me, asking if everything is okay. I burst through the exit and onto the street and see her walking down the sidewalk, away from the building. I jog until she's in hearing range and call after her. "Syd! Stop!"

This only causes her to pick up her pace, which pushes my jog into a run until I'm close enough to reach out and grab her arm. I stop and spin her around. "Sydney, please stop!"

Her face is flushed an angry red, and her eyes are on fire as she looks down at my hand and then directly at me. She growls at me through clenched teeth. "Let go of my arm right now, Justin."

I open my hand and release it but move to step in front of her, blocking her way. "Syd, talk to me. What are you doing here? Do you know how happy I am to see you?" I try to pull her into my arms, but she shoves me away.

"Do not touch me!" She paces around in a circle and then stops in front of me, her hands shaking by her side. "I came to surprise you. I had a meeting at the publishing house today and wanted to surprise you." She sneers and throws her hands up in the air. "Guess I'm the one who got the surprise, huh?"

I shake my head, frustrated that she pulls away every time I try to touch her. "Syd, what are you talking about?"

Her eyes land on mine, wide and wild. "The song, Justin? The one you were just singing? Those are my words. That was my poem!"

Fuck. My pulse pounds at the speed of light. *She heard me singing the fucking song.* Every internal battle I waged with myself over whether to tell her is instantly lost when I see what my secret has done to her. I try to reach for her hand again, wanting, needing the comfort of her touch as I try to explain, and flinch when she yanks it from my grasp.

"Were you even going to tell me? How did you even get it? I never showed it to you, to anyone!"

"Syd, can we go somewhere else and talk about this? Back to my loft. Let's go someplace more quiet and private." I look around at the people on the sidewalk staring at us as they walk by.

"Just tell me, Justin!" She's yelling now, and I'm so afraid that she's going to leave that I force her into my arms, locking them around her as she squirms against me to get loose. "Let me go!"

"Syd, Syd, please. Please, stop yelling and let me try to explain." I'm desperate and at a loss but feel a sense of relief when she stops moving and relaxes against me. It lasts for only a second, though, when I hear the next words out of her mouth.

"Please, let me go. Please." She's pleading, something she's never had to do before with me, and it sends a shock through my entire body. I immediately let go of her and step away, my hands scraping through my scalp as I scramble to figure out my next step. A small dash of hope washes over me when she doesn't walk away.

"Sydney, can I take you home and explain? Please?" It's the first time I've stopped long enough to think about her, instead of myself, and leave this decision up to her.

She nods and turns, walking back in the direction of the studio. "I left my suitcase in the building. I need to get it."

"Yeah, okay. Of course." I keep in step beside her but make sure to respect her space and don't try to reach for her. We gather her bag, my guitar, and after explaining to Andrea that I need to go deal with some personal stuff, we exit the building.

"It's about a twenty-minute walk to my place, or I can call an Uber if you want?"

"Let's walk." She looks to me for direction, so I gently take the suitcase from her, turn toward home, and start walking. After ten minutes of silence, she finally speaks.

"Justin, were you going to tell me?" Her voice is soft, no longer full of anger but so obviously full of hurt.

"I swear, I was." I rush through my next words, trying to explain. "I found your notebook at your apartment one night when I couldn't sleep. I was so blown away by your words, your thoughts, your talent. You'd never shown me anything except the little love notes you'd left for me." I take a deep breath and surge forward. "That poem, the one you wrote about me, it slayed me. When I read it, music for it just started pouring out of me, and the next thing I knew, I had turned it into a song."

"But why didn't you tell me?" She was trying so hard to understand, but I know that I hadn't said anything that made any sense yet.

"The song was supposed to just be for you. I was going to sing it at Kelly's wedding as a surprise."

She looks over at me and gives me the first glimpse of a smile that I've seen since I laid eyes on her in the studio, and it makes my stomach jump in hope.

"I was playing around with some other stuff you had written, and Andrea heard—"

She stops mid-stride and cuts me off. "Wait, there's more? You took other poems?"

I nod my head reluctantly, realizing I just took three huge steps backward from any hope of forgiveness with her. She shakes her head; I think to try to keep her anger at bay. "How many more?"

"*'Choices'* and *''Til the End',*" I say quietly. She begins walking again so I do as well. She doesn't say anything, so I keep talking in hopes of explaining. "Andrea heard me playing around with *"Choices,"* and he went absolutely crazy for it. Said it had everything it needed to get me on the charts, so I played "In Your Arms," too, and I thought he was going to have a stroke he loved it so much. I know I should have told you as soon as he heard the songs. I don't know why I didn't. But I swear, I would have, Sydney. You know I would never have released them without your permission."

She stops again and turns toward me, her eyes misty, her voice low when she speaks. "But, Justin, you stole my words. Those were mine. You should have asked me."

I shake my head, knowing she is right. Knowing what I did was wrong, no matter the reason. There's nothing more I can say to defend myself, so I do the only other thing I can think of, and I apologize. "I'm so sorry, Sydney. Truly. I don't know how it went so far without me telling you. It started out innocently enough, but I knew as soon as Andrea asked me to record the songs that it was wrong. I'll pull them and tell him we can't use them. I'm sorry, so, so sorry, Sydney. I fucked up."

I take a step closer to her and find the courage to cradle her face in my hands and place a tender kiss on her trembling lips. "Just, please, please tell me that we can get past this. I can't lose you, Syd. Not over this."

One of her hands covers mine as a single tear falls out of the corner of her eye, splitting my heart in two as I watch it cut a trail down her cheek. "Don't you know that I would have given them to you, Justin? I would have given you the whole notebook if you had asked. Just like I gave you my heart."

CHAPTER SEVENTEEN

I fly home the next day, my heart still wary but with some peace made between us. On the plane ride home, I replay the previous evening in my head and hope I've made the correct choice. I don't ask for much; at least, I don't think I do, but I do ask that a person be honest with me. He lied to me, and he stole from me. Yes, I would have given him the poems if he asked, but he didn't.

We stayed in, and he ordered take-out for us, a foreign concept where we're from; no delivery options unless you live in one of the larger cities. He tried so hard to make me feel comfortable and bent over backward to meet my every need, but I felt hollow inside. The only time I felt anything was in the desperate lovemaking we made during the night. It was like we were both clinging to the one lifeline we knew was still intact.

In reality, I didn't need to fly home until tomorrow, but I need some space to think about and process what happened. I know in my heart that Justin is a good man, an amazing man. And, yes, he's absolutely an honest man. So many times, I've heard that the entertainment industry will chew you up and spit you out a completely different person. He'd been in New York City less than two weeks, and already this decision by him, that I don't think he would have made before, sits between us now.

The more I run it around and around in my head, the sicker I feel. I place my hand over my stomach and take a few breaths, waiting for the moment to pass, but when I sense it's getting worse, I unfasten my seatbelt and bolt for the lavatory, just shutting the door in time before I throw up in the blue airline water.

The splash makes me gag, and I throw up again, this time clenching my eyes tight to try to block out the view. I reach up blindly, close the lid, and then find the button to flush the toilet as a knock sounds at the door. "Are you okay, ma'am. Can I help at all?"

"I'm okay. Thank you. Maybe some water?" I call back through the door.

"Of course."

I rinse my mouth, splash cold water on my face, pat it dry, and then pull the lever to open the door. The flight attendant is waiting outside with a bottle of water. "Here you go. You sure you're okay?"

I nod my head and take the water gratefully. "Yes, yes, I'll be fine. Thank you." I make my way back to my seat and sip on some of the water before falling into a restless sleep.

Two hours later, I jolt awake and look out the window as the plane lands on the runway, a sigh of relief leaving me at being home again. I called Kelly before I took off, telling her what happened, and am so happy to find her waiting with open arms as I walk out of the arrivals terminal.

"You okay?" She holds me for a minute then releases me, grabbing my suitcase out of my hand.

"Yeah." I look at her and shrug. "I mean, I can't stop loving him for this, right? But I do think I can be disappointed for a little bit."

"Hell yes, you can." She's my constant cheerleader and number one support team. "If you had called me yesterday, I may have jumped on a plane and kicked his ass myself."

I chuckle and link my arm through hers, resting my head on her shoulder as we walk out to the parking lot. "I love you, Kell."

"I'm hard not to love," she counters back smugly. Her head turns and she looks at me. "You feel okay, though? You don't look so great."

"I puked on the plane! It was so gross! That blue water splashed up everywhere and made me gag even more." I scrunch my face up in disgust at the memory.

"You get drunk last night?" She laughs jokingly.

"We didn't drink a drop. Wasn't that kind of night after everything, ya know?"

"Maybe you're pregnant! Wouldn't that be a kick in the ass?" She slaps playfully at my arm as she unlinks it to unlock the car.

My mind starts racing at her words, and I try to remember the last time I had my period. I stop breathing when I realize I can't remember. "Oh no."

Kelly stops what she's doing and looks at me, brows furrowed. "What?"

"I can't remember the last time I had my period."

Her mouth drops open in a wide O as what I said registers. "I was totally kidding, Syd!"

"I know, but, Kelly, what if I am pregnant?" Panic makes my voice shaky as I ask.

"Well, there's only one way to find out, right?" She throws my bag in the back seat and tells me to get in the car. "Let's go get a test."

I get in and look over at her, fear in my eyes, and begin chewing my nails. *Shit, shit, shit.* I think back to all the times I had sex with Justin over the summer, which was a ton, but can only think of twice that we didn't use protection. Once was in the hayloft, but that was a few months ago. Have I had my period since then? I smile as I remember that day; it was the day we told each other I love you.

The only other time was at the pond a few weeks ago. I scour my brain trying to remember if I had my period between the two times we didn't use protection but come up blank. Kelly pulls into the pharmacy, and seeing my state, tells me to wait in the car. She's back within ten minutes and hands me a bag. I look inside and find five different tests, and look over at her with raised brows.

She shrugs in defense. "I didn't know which one to get, but you can bet ole Martha's gonna be spreading some pregnancy rumors about me this week. Good thing I'm getting married in two weeks."

I laugh weakly, knowing for sure that I'm not getting married in two weeks, so if I am pregnant, I'm screwed. She parks at my apartment a few minutes later, and we both hustle up the stairs and inside. Simba pounces off the counter and runs between my legs in greeting, almost knocking me over. I reach down and scratch his head and then head straight to the bathroom with the bag of tests.

I rip open three of them and read the directions for each one. *I have to try and hold them in my stream of urine as I pee?* Good lord, that's going to be hard with three sticks. I open the door and yell to Kelly to bring me a solo cup. She's handing it to me through the door in five seconds flat, and I laugh to myself as I shut the door, contemplating the various uses a solo cup is good for. I squat, pee in the cup, and then dip each one in the urine until it's covered.

I carry the three tests out to the kitchen and line them up on the counter. Kelly looks at me and then at the clock. "How long do you have to wait?"

"It said three to five minutes."

"Three of the longest damn minutes of our lives," she wails.

"Tell me about it, Kell! What if I'm actually pregnant?" I shriek back at her, my nerves finally breaking.

"If you're pregnant, we'll deal with it. Let's just wait and see what the tests say."

My phone dings from my purse, so I walk over to grab it and see Justin has sent me a text to check if I've made it home okay.

I send him a text back.

-Just got home. I'll call you tonight. Xo

-Okay. I love you. Are you sure we're okay?

"Fuck." Kelly's voice tears my gaze away from my phone and over to her. She's holding up all three tests, a look of horror on her face. I step closer and feel my heart stop in my chest when I look at the results. One has two bright pink lines, one has a bright plus sign, and the other states in bold, capital letters, POSITIVE.

"Fuck is right."

I look back at my phone, type Justin a one-word response, and then fall spectacularly apart.

-Positive

I READ HER TEXT AND SHAKE MY HEAD. THIS MAY BE THE shortest text conversation in history between us. They are usually filled with more Xs and Os and lots of love words in between. I royally fucked up. I know she said she forgives me, and I know she said I can use the poems on the demo if I want, but now, it doesn't feel right.

I'm at the studio and need to make a decision. I explain it to Andrea and hope he understands, because I've got plenty of songs I haven't even played for him yet. Some of them will work for the sound he thinks we need. I pull my hat off my head and run my fingers through my hair, noting I need to find a place to get it cut before Kelly's wedding next week.

"Hey, my man!" Andrea strolls in and plunks himself down on

the chair across from me, his knee bopping a mile a minute again. I stare at it and wonder where the hell this guy gets so much damn energy. "I've got some fabulous news for you!"

I smile weakly, knowing I don't have the same for him. "What's up?"

"You're going to Hollywood!" he yells, sounding like one of the judges from "American Idol" and I give him an empty stare in return, confusion entering the equation.

"Say what?"

He jumps out of the seat and claps me on the shoulder, his grin growing even wider. "I just got off the phone with the mothership! They want to sign you! They want to see you next week out in L.A.!"

I shake my head, making sure I heard him clearly, excitement growing in my chest. "What? Are you fucking kidding me?"

"No way, man! This is for real!" I watch as he paces around, his hands waving around as he talks. "I sent them the rough cut of "Fridays" and "Choices" you played yesterday morning, and they gobbled the shit up! They said they want you now, before someone else grabs you up."

My stomach plummets when I digest the words coming out of his mouth. "Fridays" and "Choices?" The songs I want him to pull. "Did you play anything else for them?" I hold out hope that he did.

"Sure, sure, man, but those are the songs that pushed it over the edge for them. They loved the sound of them." He sits back across from me and whips out his phone. "Okay, so we have to fly out on Thursday, meet with them Friday, and then record a few of the songs in their studio over the weekend."

"I can't go next weekend," I respond quickly. "It's the wedding. I told you I have to go back home for that."

"Man! It's the fucking mothership of all recording labels. If they tell you to come, you come." His eyes are wide in disbelief that I'm even arguing about this. "I mean, you're not in the wedding or anything, right? I'm sure they'll understand. I mean, shit, your girl supports you, right?"

His mention of Sydney brings back up the other topic I know I need to discuss with him. "Yeah, listen, Andrea, about the songs, she actually wrote them. I'm not sure I'm going to use them anymore."

His knee stops bouncing, and for the first time since I've known him, a serious look crosses his face. "She doesn't want you to use them, or you don't want to use them?"

I shrug, not sure if there's a difference anymore. "I don't know, man. She said I can use them, but ya know, they're her words, and I'm just not sure I'm feeling them anymore."

"Well, you better get to feeling them again." He stands up and begins pacing. "That's what they want, and if she said you can use them, there's no conflict. I mean, it might be a little sticky with the label. They want to sell you as a singer/songwriter, but hey, we'll make sure she gets a cut of anything you make on the songs, okay?"

I sigh and put my head in my hands as I listen to him go on about how it's going to be okay, how we'll work it all out, and all I can see is Sydney's face when she saw me singing her song. It's a look I never want to see on her face again. I pick my head up and cut off his rambling. "Just see what you can do about moving the date, okay. If I miss this wedding, Sydney's going to fucking kill me. She's coming back here with me after the wedding, so I need to drive with her."

He waves his hand at me dismissively, nodding his head. "Yeah, yeah, I'll see what I can do."

It turns out he couldn't do much. The label has a tight schedule and apparently already moved heaven and earth to make time in the studio for me next weekend. I know I've gotta call Syd and try to explain, and also try to figure out how and when I can fly out so I can drive back with her to Brooklyn, but I'm scared as hell.

I finally pick up the phone, two days later, and call her. When she picks up, music is blaring in the background and I can barely hear her.

"Hello?" I yell into the phone.

"Justin?" More music and loud noise. I look at the time, and it suddenly dawns on me that she's at Kelly's bachelorette party. "One second. I'm going somewhere I can talk!"

I wait and finally hear her voice, background noise gone. "Justin? Can you hear me now?"

"Yeah. Hey, babe. Sorry, I forgot about the party," I say quietly.

"I figured, but you haven't called in a couple days, so…" She trails off, I'm sure waiting for me to fill in the blank about why I haven't called.

"Yeah, sorry. Andrea's working me like a dog at the studio, and you said you wanted a little space, so I thought…" I try lamely.

"Justin, we're a thousand miles apart. I think that's plenty of space." I can hear the hurt in her voice, and it slices through me like a knife. "I've had plenty of space. I can't wait to see you next week."

My stomach clenches as the next words tumble out. "Yeah, about that. I have some good news and some bad news."

I wait for her to say something, but all I get is silence, so I continue. "Andrea played my tracks to one of the big labels and they are really interested. They want to sign me." I try to put some excitement into my announcement, but honestly, all I feel is scared of how she's going to react next.

"That's amazing, babe. I'm so happy for you!" Her voice is full of joy at my news, and I cringe when the next words fly from my mouth.

"But, Syd, they need me in L.A. next weekend to record some of the tracks. It's the only time they have on the books."

"Next weekend? Like, Kelly's wedding weekend?" All excitement is gone.

"Babe, I tried like hell to get another date, but they insist it has to be next weekend."

"Tell them no." Her voice is firm and matter-of-fact.

"I can't tell them no. What if this is my only chance?"

"Justin, it won't be your only chance. You cannot miss the wedding. I need you here next weekend. We have things we need to talk about. Big things."

I sigh, already wary that my career is putting me in this position. "I know. I know. We have lots we need to talk about, babe, and we will. I promise. I'm going to fly straight home from L.A., and we can drive back here and talk the entire ride to Brooklyn."

"No."

I rear back in surprise at the tone of her voice. "No?"

"I need you here. It's important, Justin. More than you realize. Tell them no. If they really want you, they'll find another date."

I stammer out my confusion. "Syd, I can't tell them no. It doesn't work like that."

"It needs to work like that, Justin. You need to make a choice. Me or them."

I'm stunned at her response. I mean, I knew she was going to be mad, but I didn't expect this level of anger or these demands from her. She's *always* supported me and my dreams.

"Syd, it's you. You know, it's always you. Please, try to understand," I plead.

"I wouldn't ask if it wasn't important." Her voice is shaky, and I know she's about to cry. I think she's also realizing that I won't be able to give her what she's asking.

"I'll be there two days after the wedding. I promise. You're going to be so busy helping bridezilla that you won't even notice I'm not there, okay? And we're going to be together after that, every day."

"Justin, please, I'm begging you." She's crying now, and I shake my head in disgust at myself. I hate making her feel this way.

"Two days, baby. Just add two more days to our count. It's not that much longer." In response, I can only hear her sniffling and weeping quietly. "Syd, talk to me."

She clears her throat and then finally responds. "I've gotta go. Bye, Justin."

"Wait, Syd! I don't want to hang up like this!" I'm almost yelling now in desperation.

"I'm at Kelly's party. I have to go." She sighs heavily.

"Wait, wait!" I can't hang up like this. "Have I told you lately that I love you?"

Her voice cracks, and she scoffs. "Bye, Justin," is her only response before the line goes dead.

CHAPTER EIGHTEEN

Ten days later, I push through the front door to Hook's, surprised to see Kelly standing behind the bar.

"You're late, asshole." She's glaring at me, and I know I'm in for so much shit. "Where the hell have you been?"

"Aren't you supposed to be on your honeymoon?" I respond dryly. I'm so not in the mood for this.

"Next week. Remember, we delayed it so we wouldn't be exhausted after the wedding?" She moves down and under the bar so she can be on the same side as me. "You really didn't listen to anything Sydney told you, did you?"

I roll my eyes. "Where is she, Kelly?"

She raises her arms and shrugs, playing dumb. "Who?"

I take two steps closer to her, my patience getting short. "Don't play coy with me. Where's Sydney? I went to the apartment, and it's empty, and all my calls go straight to voicemail."

"A whole week? Isn't that right around the time you told her no? When you told her you wouldn't come back for my wedding, even though she begged you?" She's jabbing her finger into my chest at the end of each question, and it hurts. I reach down and push it away.

"Cut the shit, Kelly. I told her why I couldn't come."

"Yeah, I heard all about it." She scrunches up her eyes and mouth. "As she cried on my damn shoulder. Two days, two more days." She pokes me in the chest. "It's been five, Justin. Five days!"

I blow out a frustrated breath and step back from her to stop the relentless poking. "I couldn't help it. They wouldn't let me leave."

"Wouldn't let you leave?" she spits back at me. "You're a grown ass man. If you want to leave, you just leave!"

"I didn't have a choice. If I'd have left, I would have lost the record deal." I plead.

She scoffs and throws me a glance that in no way shows any sympathy. "Well, now, you've lost a whole lot more, haven't you?"

My pulse pounds harder. "What's that supposed to mean?"

She turns and faces me, a look of complete contempt on her face. "You made your choice, Justin. Now, she's made hers."

"What the fuck is that supposed to mean?" I repeat, angry now, or maybe just afraid, and my skin breaks out in a cold sweat.

"She's gone," she states matter of fact, like she's telling me it's raining out.

"Gone?" I repeat, making sure I heard her correctly.

"Gone. G.O.N.E. Gone." She spells it out this time. I seriously want to choke her right now, but I need more answers.

"Gone where?"

"I guess, if she wants you to know, she'll call you." She spins around and walks back under the bar, which is probably a good thing, because I'm damn close to wrapping my hands around her neck and squeezing until she tells me where Syd is. "Oh, wait. She can't call you, because after she hung up on you, she threw her damn phone against a wall. Might be why she's not answering any of your calls, too."

I lift my brows in surprise, knowing Syd isn't one to lose her temper like that. I'll have to get her a new phone. I turn my attention back to Kelly. "You're seriously not going to tell me where she is?" I'm shaking inside. This can't be happening. I know I'm late, but I'm here. We can start our life together now.

"Nope," she sing-songs across the bar.

"Thanks a fucking lot, Kelly," I spit back, no longer caring if I piss her off.

"You're welcome." Her face turns angry now. "Now, get the fuck out of my bar."

I know she's not kidding, so I spin and stomp out of the bar, slamming the door behind me as I leave. "Fuck!" I scream loudly as I stand on the sidewalk, several people jumping when I do. I scowl at all of them, not giving one ounce of shit, and make my way to my truck. I climb in and drive to her father's house next. I'm scared as hell to face him, but it's the only other place I think she might be.

When I arrive, I frown. Her car isn't in the drive, but I suppose she could be out running errands, so I get out of the truck and go knock on the front door. After a couple minutes, the door swings open, her dad in the doorway.

"You." He shakes his head and frowns. "Guess you better come in."

I follow him inside to the living room where he sinks back into his usual recliner. "So, what do you have to say for yourself?"

Jesus, I thought Kelly was going to be tough. This is about a thousand times harder. I clear my throat and move to sit on the couch across from him. I'm surprised when I look down and see Simba twining in and out of my legs, purring loudly. My heart jolts in hope. "Is Sydney here, sir?"

He looks around and then back at me. "Do you see her anywhere?"

I raise my brows and rear back. *Shit. Way harder than Kelly.* I start again. "I know I missed the wedding. I know she's obviously really mad, but I'm here now. I just want to find her so I can fix this and we can go back to Brooklyn."

"Son, I don't think she's going back to Brooklyn with you." He presses his fingers into a steeple, resting his chin on it lightly, his eyes growing a little soft. "She made me promise not to tell you where she has gone, and as much as it pains me to see that look on your face right now, I have to honor my daughter's wishes."

She's not coming to Brooklyn with me? She doesn't want me to know where she is? My heart is racing, along with my mind, and I shake my head in disbelief. "Wh—what?"

I watch him rise and leave the room, unable to make myself get up, because if I do, it means I'm done. I don't know where to go next. He comes back and sets a guitar case on the table in front of me, pointing to it. "She said to give this to you."

I stare at the case in front of me, completely dumbfounded, and then up at her dad, who shrugs. "I don't know, son. I figured you would know."

Leaning forward, I finger the hard guitar case and then flip the three locks holding it closed, raising the lid. My breath catches in my throat when I see what's inside. It's a Martin HD28E acoustic guitar, the retro version, with light wood grain coloring and a gorgeous dark mahogany neck with pearl inlays between the frets. I strum my fingers across the strings, the sound of the notes vibrating against my skin, and look wide-eyed to her dad. "What is this?"

His brows raise. "A guitar?"

It's a guitar, all right. It's *the* guitar of guitars. She asked me once, if I could have any guitar in the world, which one would it be? This is the one I told her about. I played it once at a store during a trip to Nashville, and holding it, hearing the music it produced, was better than any wet dream I'd ever had. She laughed when I told her that. I smile at the memory but then frown when I turn and look back at the guitar.

"She said to make sure I gave it to you if you came here. That's all she told me." I watch as he settles himself back into his chair.

I swipe my hand quickly across my cheek and look down to hide my face from her dad as I realize tears have begun to fall. I blindly snap the locks on the case and rise, grabbing the handle as I do to take it with me. I sniffle and clear my throat. "Will you tell her I came for her? And will you ask her to call me?"

Her dad stands again and nods. "I'll tell her."

I walk to the door and am about to push through it but turn back. "I love her, Mr. Porter."

"I know you do, Justin. But this is up to her now."

I nod my head in response, and I suppose in goodbye, and then head back out to my truck and drive to my cottage. When I arrive, I carry the case inside and set it on the coffee table in front of me as I sit. I flip the locks, lift the lid, and then sit there for hours staring at it, as every memory of us plays through my mind. I can't believe she bought this for me. I know for a fact it runs around four grand, so she must have used some of her advance to do it. She told me she was going to use her advance to pay off her student loans.

Finally lifting it from the case, I set it in my lap, freezing when I see what lays in the bottom of the case. I reach my hand in and pull the notebook, her notebook, out and blow out a shaky breath. I put the guitar back in the case and lay the notebook flat across my lap. I'm terrified to open the pages. I don't know what I'm going to find, and while every cell in my being wants to know, there's a huge part of me that knows this is the end.

Once I finally get the nerve to lift it from my lap, I set it back on top of the guitar and walk away. I'm not ready for this yet. I strip down to my boxers and slide into our bed, the bed I shared with her for almost four months. I roll over and squeeze the pillow that she always rested her head on and inhale deeply. Her scent still lingers in the fabric, so I cling to it, wrapping it in my arms tightly. Then, I finally break down, sobs wracking my body until I eventually fall into an exhausted sleep.

I pick my new cell phone up off the table and look at the screen to see who's calling. I mean, I've only given four people this number: Kelly, my dad, my literary agent, and my publisher. The options are limited in who it could be.

"Hi, Dad," I say after pressing the green accept call option.

"Hey, sweets. You doing okay down there?" I can hear the concern and worry in his voice, and I pray again that I've made the right choice, pray Justin will make the right choice, as I look out at the blue ocean waves rolling on the shore outside.

"I'm good, Daddy. Auntie Wendy is taking good care of me."

"She was always my favorite. After your mom, of course." He chuckles, making sure I understand that my mom always came first. He never made it a secret, though, that her younger sister, my Auntie Wendy, was his favorite. For a really long time, she lived in Australia, so seeing her wasn't a common thing, but when we did, it was always a treat. They named me after her; well, kind of. She was living in Sydney when I was born and insisted that my mom name me after her, but my mom didn't want another Wendy, so Sydney it was.

"He came to the house today, Sydney." My heart stills in my chest, my blood running cold as I absorb his words. "He's taking this really, really hard."

I'm nodding my head, unable to speak yet as I try to control the tears that are now running down my cheeks. "Are you sure this is what you want, honey? It's obvious you both love each other, and well, do you really want to be alone right now?"

I blink my eyes until I can see clearly again and finally squeak back a reply. "I've made my decision, and now, it's up to him to make his."

"Well, I'm not sure if I agree with you after seeing him today, but I'll respect your choice."

"Did you give him the guitar?" I ask quietly.

"I did. He seemed surprised." I know my dad's trying to get more out of me, but I don't have it in me to explain. I think he thought it was one that Justin already owned and left behind, not understanding it was a gift I bought for him.

"Did he open it? Take it out of the case?" I question further.

"Well, he opened it, but no, he just looked at it and then buckled it up and left."

A small piece of me dies, and I wonder if he'll pick the guitar up and play it. If he doesn't, he won't see what I've left him. But it's another choice I have to live with. Part of my decision in finding out if I'm enough.

"Okay, thanks, Dad."

"Sydney, you can still come home." His comment sounds more like a suggestion, and I appreciate his support, more than he knows, but it's not something I can do right now.

"I know, Dad. Thanks. I'm going to go, okay?"

"Okay, sweetie. Say hi to Wendy."

"I will. Love you, Dad."

"Love you, too."

We end the call, which for me also signifies the end of my relationship with Justin. Unless he opens the notebook.

CHAPTER NINETEEN

TWO YEARS LATER

I take a deep breath and push through the door of Hook's Landing, not sure who or what I'll find inside, but nervous none the less. It's a Thursday, and it's early in the afternoon, so I'm not expecting a big crowd. I planned it this way on purpose. Everywhere I go now, I'm recognized and mobbed by fans wanting an autograph, a picture, a piece of me to take home with them. It's exhausting and not the part of fame I was expecting when I became successful.

I sigh in relief when I step inside and only see one person sitting at the bar, and then groan in frustration when I realize it's Kelly. She spins around as the bell above the door sounds, her face widening in surprise when her eyes land on me.

"What in the world are you doing here, Mr. Fancy Pants?" She rises from the stool and saunters in my direction, crossing her arms as she approaches.

I pull my sunglasses off, forgetting that they're on my nose for a moment as they've become a regular fixture in trying to conceal myself from the public eye. I give her a lopsided smile and shrug. "Hey, Kelly. Nice to see you, too."

She stops in front of me and shakes her head in disbelief. "What's it been, two years?"

Actually, it's been twenty months and eighteen days since I walked out of this bar, but who's counting? "Yeah, something like that. How've you been?"

"Just dandy. You?" she fires back, feisty as always.

"Oh, you know, just living the dream." More like a fucking nightmare, but there's no way in hell I'm telling her that. It's been two years of endless tours, and writing, and recording, with not one moment to catch my breath. On one hand, it's been a great way to bury my head in the sand and avoid my shattered heart, but on the other, I've not had one moment to try to fix it. Until now.

"Oh yeah, I heard you moved to L.A. Living the Cali life now. Got your picture on the cover of *Us* and everything. How's it feel being the sexist man in America?" Her tone is condescending, and she's definitely not looking for an answer from me, so I don't give her one.

"Has Sydney been around?" I fiddle with the sunglasses in my hands. I can't believe it's been almost two years and she's never called me.

She shakes her head and lets out a long breath, and for the first time, I actually see something in her attitude toward me shift. She frowns. "She doesn't live here anymore. You know that, right?"

"I didn't know, actually. I don't know anything. All I know is she cut off all ties to me after I missed your wedding." I shrug, hoping she'll give me more information if I don't try to pry so hard from her.

"There's a big part of me that really wants to tell you, Justin."

"But?" I know there's a but coming by the sad look on her face. Or maybe it's pity. I'm not sure, but I know it's no longer anger.

"But she would kill me. If she wants to see you, she'll find you. It's not like it's that difficult."

"Does she want to see me?" I grasp at any piece of hope I might be able to get.

She shifts her feet and shrugs again. "I honestly don't know, but between you and me, I wish she would. I'm tired of being the one you have to come to every time you want to find her."

And there's the girl I know so well, back again to make me feel so good about myself. I roll my eyes and then pull an envelope out of my back pocket. "Will you give this to her whenever you see her again?"

She looks at it, snags it out of my hand, and walks over to the bar, placing it on the counter.

"Don't lose it, okay? It's important." I stress, concerned that she's just leaving it up on the bar.

"Yeah, I've got it," she says dismissively. She turns her head toward the back of the room as a cry sounds out, then darts her eyes back to me. My eyes move in the direction of the crying and open wide when I see a baby nestled in a swing in the back corner.

"Kelly, you have a baby?" I grin in surprise. "In a bar?"

"Shut up, Justin." She scurries to where the baby is and pulls it gently from the swing, cooing as she does. I'm stunned into silence, watching Kelly actually be loving and kind to the little bundle in her arms. I walk closer so I can get a look as she rocks it back and forth in her arms.

I smile when I see the round head full of short, curly blonde locks and bright blue eyes staring back at me, a wet, slippery thumb making its way in and out of the baby's mouth. I reach out with my finger and laugh when the little hand catches it and clings on with a firm grip. "Why, Kelly, I'm shocked you made something this cute! What's the little monster's name?"

She looks over at me, sticking her tongue out but with laughter in her eyes. "We call her Tini. She was born five weeks early and was only five pounds, and the teeny, tiniest thing you ever did see."

"She's beautiful." She's still got a death grip on my finger, but I enjoy every second of her hold on me. "She's gonna be a heartbreaker. Look at those eyes!" I look up at Kelly, who's staring at me, like a deer caught in the head lights. I frown and then look back at the baby, cooing softly to her.

"Do you want to hold her?" The question comes out as a surprise, as if she can't believe I actually like babies.

"Can I?" I ask excitedly, already sliding my sunglasses into my shirt pocket, freeing up my other hand so I can take her. She hands her over to me, looking a little nervous as she does, and steps back, keeping her eyes glued to both of us.

I'm in complete awe as Tini stares back at me, beautiful lids covered in long lashes blinking as she tilts her head as if trying to decipher who I am. I smile back at her and begin gently rocking her and then humming. She gurgles back at me and smiles, I think in approval of the music, so I sing softly to her.

> *"Can't tell if you're eyeing me the irony it gets to me*
> *tape my mouth and lie to me I can't speak*
> *And I drink before you calm down the nerves*
> *Why can't I just be myself around her*
> *In your arms I feel safe*
> *But you try to keep me awake*
> *then I go and sleep tight."*

"UGH, JUSTIN, REALLY?" I LIFT MY HEAD AND LOOK questioningly at Kell.

"I know it went to number one and all, but it's the song you stole from her!" She places her hand on her hip and gives me a look that says, 'duh'.

"And every time I sing it, it reminds me what it felt like when she was in my arms," I state it flatly, and then turn my attention back to the baby, continuing to sing the song where I left off. When I finish, I raise my head and see Kelly holding her phone up. I lift my eyebrow suspiciously as she shifts it down quickly.

"She really is a beauty, Kell. Congrats to you and Adam." I walk back and transfer the baby from my arms to her. "How old is she?"

"Just a little over a year," she answers between coos to the baby.

"Honeymoon baby, huh?" I wink at her playfully.

"Yeah, I guess." She looks at me again, her eyes boring into mine, making me feel uncomfortable, so I take it as my queue to leave.

I pull the sunglasses from my pocket, sliding them on, and start for the door. "It was," I pause for a minute, thinking of the right word to use, "interesting to see you, Kell."

"Yeah, that's one word for it," she retorts, a short laugh following.

I turn back to her before I pull the door open. "Kell? Will you tell her I kept my old cell? I never turn it off. If she wants to call."

She nods her head once, and I turn and walk out of the bar.

I TAKE A DEEP BREATH AND PUSH THROUGH THE DOOR OF HOOK'S Landing, dreading the conversation I need to have with Kelly. I know she's going to be more upset than I am, and dealing with an emotional Kelly is never fun.

"Hey, I'm back," I call out, seeing no one in the front area of the bar. I look at my watch and note the time; just after two-thirty.

"Back here! I'm changing Tini," she calls from the bathroom. "Be right out. Almost done!"

I walk over to the bar and plop myself on a stool, throwing my purse down on the bar. I'm so tired. Physically, mentally, more than I know if I can handle tired. I scrub my hands over my face and force a smile when I hear Kelly's footsteps coming down the hallway from the bathrooms. She's holding a smiling Tini, and I get up quickly to greet them.

"How's my little angel?" I take her from Kelly's arms and snuggle her against me as her tiny arms wrap around my neck.

"Mamma!" she squeals.

"Yes, Mommy's back." I shift her so I can see her round little face and plant kisses all over her cheeks, giggles pouring from her cherub lips as I do. *God, I love this little girl.* I glance over and stop when I see Kelly staring wide-eyed at me. "What?"

"Okay, I have to tell you something, but I don't want you to freak out, but I know you're going to, so now I'm freaking out."

"Jesus Christ on a cracker, Kelly. Just spit it out already." *Great, just what I needed, more good news today.*

"Justin was here. Like, he literally just left ten minutes ago. I was shitting my pants, praying you didn't come back while he was here," she blurts out, her face getting pinker as she does.

I reach blindly for a chair, needing to sit down immediately as my legs turn to jelly, and drop into it, resting the baby on my lap. "Did he see Tini?" It's the first thought that races through my mind.

She nods her head violently, wringing her hands together. "Uh-huh, but don't worry! He thought she was mine."

Holy shit. I've been wondering if this day would actually come, and now that it has, I wasn't even here for it. I swing my head back to her. "What did he want?"

"Well, you. He was looking for you. And for crying out loud, he was so pathetic, I actually felt sorry for him and wanted to tell him everything."

My eyes fly to hers, wide.

"No! No! Don't worry, I didn't." She walks over to the bar, grabs something off it, and then hands it to me. "He told me to give this to you." She hands me an envelope and then frowns. "Syd, do you think maybe it's time you called him? I mean, he's here! That has to mean something. And, I mean, you had his baby!"

I glare back at her, mostly angry because I've asked myself these very same questions a hundred times in the last year. "He made his choice, Kelly. I'm just giving him what he wants." I turn back to the envelope, my name scribbled across the front in his handwriting, and lift the baby, handing her off to Kelly. I rip it open and pull out... a check? I read it and gasp when I see the amount and then look up at Kell. "This is a check for five-hundred-thousand dollars! Made out to me!"

Kelly snatches it out of my hand, reading it for herself, her mouth falling open as she scans the front and the back, the baby bouncing on her hip. "Shut up! This is half a million freaking dollars, Syd!"

I snatch the check out of her hand and read the fine print under the note section on the front of the paper: 'Songwriting Royalties.' He came to pay me for the songs he stole. Okay, he stole them originally, but then I told him he could have them, but he said he wasn't going to use them, but then he did anyway. I place the check on the table. "I don't want this."

"Sydney, it's a lot of money. What do you mean, you don't want it? They were your words. You deserve it."

I shake my head and then stand, taking Tini out of Kelly's arms, focusing my attention on her instead. "Have you eaten yet, little munchkin?"

I laugh when her head bops up and down, a small, toothy grin lighting up her face as she says, "Yummies!" It's her word for anything food related. I find the diaper bag in the back and pull a cookie out for her to munch on, her greedy hands latching onto it hungrily before she starts sucking on it.

"So, are you going to tell me what the doctor said?" She plops down in the chair beside me, finally broaching the subject we both have been trying to avoid.

I look over at her and try to smile bravely, even as a tear

escapes down my cheek, and I nod. "I have to start chemo next week. She said they got the tumors, but it looks like it's spread to some of my lymph nodes so this is the best way to attack it."

She clutches onto my hand, tears falling onto her cheeks now. "You know we're going to beat this, right? Treatments are so much more advanced than when your mom had it."

I nod my head, thankful for her friendship and support, and look down at the little girl in my lap, and know, more than anything, I need to fight for her.

CHAPTER TWENTY

ANOTHER TWO YEARS LATER

I stroll off the stage, giving one final wave and bow before I do, grabbing the bottle of water being handed to me by my manager as I pass. It's the last show of my tour, and the crowd was insane. I normally only do one encore, but because it's the final show, I did two. My shirt is soaked from the heat of the lighting, my throat dry, and I laugh at the irony as I guzzle the water.

"You want me to take the guitar, Justin?" It's my manager, Greg, following closely behind me as I descend the stairs off the back part of the stage.

I tighten my grip around the neck of the Martin and shake my head. "I've got it." I use it every night to play the last song of my set, "In Your Arms." It's her song, and I only play it on her guitar, which I don't let anyone else handle but me. Even though Greg knows this, he still asks me after every damn show if I want him to take the guitar.

Feeling beaten down, I'm so fucking glad this tour is over. I've been on the road for three hundred of the last three hundred and sixty-five days. Too Goddamn long. I haven't been able to write a single song, get a decent night's sleep, or see my family in over eighteen months. Sure, everyone on the road claims to be your best friend, but hell, they're just along for the ride. It's a fucking roller coaster is what it is. More dips and turns over the last twelve months than I can even remember.

I miss the days when I could walk into a bar, plug my guitar into an amp, and just sing whatever I wanted. No one grabbing at me and screaming for me to play the same song I've already played ten thousand times. No crazy fans sneaking into my room and even my bed some nights. Okay, not going to lie; sometimes, the girls were a needed relief, but no one's ever going to hold a candle or replace the only girl that's ever stolen my heart. I grimace at the thought of her, pain still rippling through my chest every time I do.

"Justin!" I hear my name being called like it is every night I walk down one of these hallways after a show, but this one has me freezing in my tracks. I whip my head in the direction it came, unable to hide my surprise when I see Sydney standing behind the roped off section of the hallway.

I do a double-take to make sure it's her. It was definitely her voice, but the hair is much shorter. This girl is much thinner than the Sydney I remember. Maybe I'm losing my mind and thinking about her is doing funny things to my head. I stare at her, and she stares back at me before a nervous smile spreads across her mouth and she gives me a short wave. *Holy shit. It's her. It's really her.*

For the first time, ever, I absentmindedly hand my guitar to Greg and float over to where she's standing. "Sydney?"

She nods her head, bottom lip stuck between her teeth, her cheeks flaring the light pink I remember so well, and I think my heart is going to explode out of my chest. I haven't seen her in almost four years. "What are you doing here?" I realize that sounds like I don't want her here, so I quickly follow it up with, "I mean, I'm thrilled to see you, but I'm just surprised!"

Before she can answer, fans realize I'm standing next to the ropes and begin to swarm the area, pushing and shoving her as they do. I reach under the rope and grab her hand, telling security it's fine, and pull her under and up against me. When I feel the outline of her ribs against my hand where I'm holding her, I look down at her in shock. *Is she fucking starving herself to death?*

I release my hold on her body and grab her hand instead, pulling her with me as I walk quickly. "Come with me." She follows beside me, almost having to jog to keep up with my fast pace. I feel her pull my hand and turn to look at her. She's red and sweating.

"Can you go a little slower, please?" She's panting and I nod, surprise washing over me again.

"Sure, sorry." I walk slower, watching to make sure she's catching her breath. "I've gotten good at running from rabid fans."

She nods and gives me a forced smile. *Shit. Why'd I go and say something stupid like that? She doesn't want to hear about my damn fans.* We finally make it to my dressing room, security opening the door as I approach, and I usher her inside before turning to lock the door. Without any thought, I turn again and plunge forward, wrapping her in my arms, a feeling of relief to finally have her there again spreading over me. "Sydney, Sydney, Sydney." I keep saying her name, I think to try to make myself believe she's really here. "I've missed you so much. So much."

Her head is nodding against me, and she's murmuring the same, her grip tight around my waist. We stay like this for several minutes; five, ten, fifteen? I'm not sure. I just know I don't want to let go of her. I'm so afraid she's going to leave again. She releases her grip around my waist first, gently pushing herself away from my body. She seems to sway once she's standing on her own, and I reach out and place my hand on her shoulder to steady her.

"You okay? You want to sit down?" I ask, concern lacing my voice.

She nods and moves to one of the couches scattered around the room. Someone pounds on the door, and I scowl. I don't want anyone bothering me right now; I don't care if the damn president is at the door. I tell her to wait for a second and storm to the door, yanking it open. "What?" I practically growl. I've never brought a woman into my damn dressing room, so I would think it would be obvious to anyone something important is happening.

Greg throws his hands up in the air as he takes a step back. "Whoa, down boy! Just want to see if you need anything!"

"Yes, I need everyone to leave me the fuck alone. Got it?" I slam the door, locking it again, and then sit beside her. I scan her from head to toe, taking in every inch of her, noting the new short hair, the way the bones jut from her collarbone, her legs—which were once so muscular but now look spaghetti thin in the tights she has on—and her lips. Her beautiful puffy pink lips are now thin and dry looking. I reach my hand out and swipe a finger tenderly over them, my eyes meeting hers, tears brimming at the edges.

I move my fingers and brush under her barely-there lashes. "Don't cry, baby. Please, don't cry. It's going to be okay."

I SHAKE MY HEAD AND THEN WRAP MY SMALL HANDS AROUND HIS large one on my face, pulling it down into my lap, and give him a sad smile. "It's not, Justin." I take a deep breath and say what I've come to tell him. "I'm sick."

His grip tightens underneath mine as his expression turns to confusion. His eyes scan over my body again, and finally, realization dawns in them. "What?"

I squeeze his hands again, needing something to hold on to as I say the words again, knowing that saying them to him will be hardest of all. "I'm sick."

He tilts his head, the corners of his eyes crinkling as he tries to absorb what I'm saying, and repeats me. "You're sick?"

I nod my head and lift one of my hands as I scoot closer to him and place it on his knee. Here comes the big one. "I have cancer."

He blinks several times, his expression stoic, then pulls his hand out of mine and stands. "Do you want a water? Or a drink?" He walks over to the small bar at one end of the room and starts rummaging through the bottles until he finds what he's looking for. "I need a drink." I watch calmly as he pours a large amount of Macallan into a glass and drinks it down in two gulps, then pours another, his hand shaking as he does.

I stand and walk over to him, his eyes following my approach, then slide the glass from his fingers and set it down on the counter. "I have things I need to say to you, and I need you to be present, okay?"

He grabs my face in his hands and looks at me, his eyes a bit wild. "You're going to be okay, though, right, Syd? You can get surgery or chemo or whatever you need, and you're going to be okay, right?"

I close my eyes, knowing if I keep looking into his, I'm going to break apart. When I shake my head, I hear him whimper and then feel his lips against mine, his tongue sweeping across my lips, the taste of the whiskey invading my mouth. I let him kiss me, and I don't stop myself from wrapping my arms around him and kissing him back because we both need this. This one moment of comfort in the worst possible moment of our lives.

His lips break away from mine, and he's peppering kisses all over my cheeks, my eyes, my nose, all while still cradling me in his large hands as he does, and I open my eyes because I feel wet drops hitting my face. I gulp back my own grief when I realize they are tears raining from his closed eyes. "I'm sorry, Justin. I'm so, so sorry."

He pulls me into his arms and holds me against him so tight, his chest vibrating as he cries. I can barely breathe from the pressure, but I don't care. Right now, right here at this moment, in his arms, I can't help but think that this wouldn't be a bad way to die. But then I picture Tini, and I know there's still so much more to say. I let him hold me until his body no longer trembles then move to extricate myself from his grip. This time, I take his hand and pull him to the couch.

"How long? How long have you been sick, Syd?" His eyes are red and swollen, a weariness to them I've never seen before.

"A little more than two years." I shut my eyes when I see him flinch, knowing he wants to know why I didn't come sooner, and then open them and continue. "It started with a lump in my breast. It was removed, but the cancer had already spread to my lymph nodes. We did chemo and radiation, but then it was in my uterus. So, they removed that and my ovaries."

"Oh my God, Sydney." He scoots closer to me and looks at me, his face a mask of pain. "Why didn't you call me? I would have come. I would have helped."

"There's nothing you could have done." I shrug sadly.

"I could have held your hand. I could have gone to the hospital with you. I would have taken care of you, Syd."

I wipe at the tears beginning to trickle from the seams of my eyes and force myself to be stronger for him. He's going to be so angry when I tell him everything. "It doesn't matter anymore because none of it worked. It's in my liver and my brain. There's nothing more that can be done."

He stands and paces back and forth in front of me. I watch, letting him absorb the news until he stops. "There has to be something else they can do. Sydney, I have so much money. I can call whoever the best is at this and get them to see you. I'm not going to let you give up."

I smile weakly, understanding his need to try to fix me, but I already know. I've accepted the reality of the situation and try to tell him just that. "There's nothing more to do. We've tried chemo and radiation, and, Justin, they can't take my brain out."

"So that's it?" His voice raises as he throws his hands in the air. "You're just going to give up? You're only twenty-seven years old, Syd!"

"I've been fighting this for two years. Believe me, I've done everything that can be done." I purse my lips together and wait for the next explosion, which he delivers as expected.

"Then what the hell are you here for?" He stops in front of me, his face flushed. "Why come here? Are you punishing me? Is this your way of getting back at me?"

I shake my head and stand on shaky legs, reaching out for his hands as I do, taking each one in mine. "There's nothing to punish you for. We've both made choices that, at the end of the day, has brought us to this very moment."

His eyes narrow as he looks down at me. "Then why? Why put me through this pain, Sydney? Why come to me now if you're just going to leave me again? I've already lost you once and it almost killed me. I don't want to do this again."

"Because we have a daughter." His whole body tightens as his eyes widen and he staggers back away from me. "You have a daughter, Justin."

CHAPTER TWENTY-ONE

I have a daughter? What the hell is she talking about?
"What?" I stumble back until I feel the wall against my back and stop. "What did you say?"

"I had a baby. Your baby, Justin. Three years ago." Her voice is even and calm, making me question if this is a dream.

"You had a baby three years ago?" I ask in disbelief. "And you're telling me it's mine?"

I watch as she nods. "She was born March twenty-fifth. Do the math. Four years ago is the summer I spent with you."

Cocking my head, I count the months backward, even though I know this isn't something she would make up. So, this means she got pregnant in June? I look at her, confusion swirling in my brain. "Did you know you were pregnant when I moved to Brooklyn?"

She shakes her head. "Not until the day I came home from seeing you in Brooklyn."

"But you got pregnant in June? How could you not have known?" I question.

"I got pregnant in August, but she came five weeks early." She walks over to me and tries to take my hand. "Will you come back and sit on the couch. I'll tell you anything you want to know."

I rip my hand from her, anger now surging through my veins. "I want to know why the hell you didn't tell me I had a daughter! Have a daughter! And she's three! How could you keep that from me, Sydney? How? I have a three-year-old daughter that I've never seen!"

She flinches at the end of each angry question I throw at her but doesn't back away from me. "Actually, you have seen her." She pulls a cell phone out of her dress pocket, scrolls through it, and then hands it to me. "Press play."

I look at her suspiciously as I take the phone and then press play. I watch as it begins and tilt my head at the memory. It's me, holding Tini in the bar, singing softly to her. I remember that day clearly. It was the last time I went looking for Syd. When the video finishes, I look at her and raise my shoulders in question. "This is Kelly's baby. Tini."

She shakes her head. "She's our baby. Kelly was watching her for me that day. You missed me by ten minutes."

"Tini's mine? My daughter?" I'm dumbstruck.

"Her name is Justine Madison. We started calling her Tini on account of how small she was when she was born, and it stuck."

I swing my head up and stare wide-eyed at her. "You named her after me?"

She gives me a small smile and nods. "It was as close as I could get to Justin Matthew. But I did give her my last name. I figured you got the first two. Plus, I don't know, the whole fame thing with you, and I didn't know what was going to happen between me and you and her."

"Do my parents know?"

"No one except my dad and Kelly's family knows about her. I left town after Kelly's wedding and didn't come back except to visit."

"Where did you go?"

"I moved to the Gulf coast. I lived with my aunt at first, and then bought my own little house after my second book was published."

As her words sink in, and the realization that I was holding my own daughter and didn't even know it registers, I stagger over to the couch and collapse onto it. A thousand thoughts are running through my head, and I don't know to process any of them. In the span of ten minutes, I found out the love of my life is dying and that I have a daughter. "How could you keep this from me?"

She moves to join me on the couch but sits so there is more distance between us now. She's quiet for a few minutes, and I'm beginning to wonder if she's going to say anything when she finally starts talking. "It's funny, that summer we were together. We loved each other so much. I never thought anything would have been able to separate us."

"You left, Syd. I didn't know where to find you."

"Justin, I told you where to find me. You never came."

I look at her, bewildered by her statement. "You never told me where to find you, and Kelly and your dad wouldn't tell me where you were. When? When did you tell me?"

"Didn't you read the notebook?"

"What notebook? Your notebook?"

Her head bounces up and down. "Yes! I put it in with the guitar I left for you."

I swing my head slowly back and forth. "Syd, I haven't opened that since I read it at your house four years ago."

"What?" Surprise ratchets the tone of her voice up three octaves. "You never read the notebook?" A look of painful realization sweeps over her face before she places her head in her hands and begins to weep. She lifts her head once to look at me, shakes it, and then begins crying harder, hiding her face again in her hands. Not sure why she's crying, and her not seemingly able to explain, I stand and go to the door.

I pull it open and ask the security guard to find Greg, and then ask him to bring the case for my Martin back here. I pace back and forth, listening to her sob, wanting to tear my damn hair out, waiting for Greg. Finally, there's a knock at the door and Greg's voice on the other side. "Justin, I've got the case."

I open the door, take the case, and give him a nod of thanks. His hand slams against the door before I can close it, and I snap my head up to find him staring back at me, brows raised, lips pursed tightly.

"What?" I ask, irritation flaring.

"You okay? You've been in there awhile."

"I'm good. Nothing for you to worry about."

"We flying out tonight, or you want to wait until morning?"

I turn my head toward the couch where Sydney's sitting, not sure how long this is going to take, and then back to him. "Better make it tomorrow morning."

He releases his hand from the door and steps back. "I'm here if you need anything. Okay? Anything at all."

I appreciate his concern and smile gratefully at him. "Thanks, man." I shut the door and then walk over to the table near the couch to open the case. Greg put the Martin back in, so I lift it out and lean it carefully against one of the chairs before lifting the notebook out of the bottom of the case.

She's quietly watching everything I'm doing, but when she sees me pull the notebook out, her eyes bug wide. "You have it with you?"

I nod. "I haven't taken it out since the first day I found it." I lean over and motion for her to take it. She stares at it, not moving. I shake it in front of her. "Take it." She reaches out slowly and takes it in her hand. "Show me."

She looks up at me, her brows creased, her lower lip clenched between her teeth, and then sets the notebook on her lap and turns the pages until she finds the last one written on. She turns the notebook around so it's facing me and then swings her gaze back up to me.

WHEN I READ THE WORDS I SCRIBBLED ON THE PAGE OF THIS notebook so very long ago, I think back to the day I wrote them and comprehend how naïve I was. Never in a million years did I think he wouldn't open the notebook and read it. How could I have left so much to chance? All the years I wasted that we could have been together. All the years I thought that us not being together was his choice. I read the words now and realize in vain how very, very stupid I was.

Justin,
Take my words, just like you took my heart
Everything I am has been yours from the start
You decide from here if we stay or part
Either way, your love I will forever impart
Xoxo
Sydney

The choice is yours.
37529 Juniper Lane
Gulf City, Florida

I WATCH HIM AS HE READS THE PAGE, TRYING TO FIGURE OUT what's going through his mind as his eyes scan back and forth. His lips press firmly together. When he finally looks up at me, his face pale, his eyes creased from frowning, he simply shakes his head and then stands up and walks to the bar. He snatches the glass of whiskey he filled earlier and takes a long swig out of it.

He turns toward me and lifts the glass in a cheering motion as a weird smile breaks across his face. "Here's to fucking up our life with one Goddamn love note." He brings the glass to his mouth and swallows what's left before slamming it back down on the counter. "Seriously? You seriously think that I *chose* not to be with you?"

I watch as he pulls the top off the bottle of Macallan and fills the glass halfway. He glances over and waves one hand in the air when he sees my concerned expression. "Oh, don't you worry. I'm fucking present. There's not enough Goddamn whiskey in this room to get me drunk enough to drown out the shit happening here right now."

He's pissed. I don't think I've ever seen him angry before. He strolls back over to me, one hand in his pocket, the other holding his drink, and stares down at me. He shrugs and scoffs. "I don't get it, Syd. I mean, fine, be pissed at me because I didn't show up to Kelly's wedding. But to be so pissed that you fucking pick up and leave the damn state? And, then, not even tell me you're having my baby? How could you keep that from me? What the hell were you thinking? Don't you know me at all? Do you want to know how badly my heart fucking bled for you? How much it hurt me to have you just disappear like that?"

I open my mouth to answer, but he shoves the hand holding the whiskey out, motioning for me to stop. "I'm so Goddamn mad at you right now." He points a shaking finger at me, yelling. "This is your fault! Yours! All this time, I thought it was me. But it was you! You did this!"

Tears run in a steady stream down my face, but I don't move to wipe them away. I know he's right, and I know nothing I can say will fix what I broke.

"Say something, Goddamn it!" I jump at the anger in his

demand and look up at him, opening my mouth to speak, but nothing comes out.

"Jesus Christ!" His fingers drag through his hair as he paces around in frustration.

I'm looking at the stupid, stupid words I wrote, so many things I wish I could go back and change swirling through my mind. I close my eyes, scrunching my lids tightly to try to block them out, and feel him sit down next to me.

"Why? Can you just tell me why, Syd?" His tone is calmer but still filled with anger as he asks.

"I thought you didn't want me. I thought you chose." I practically whisper the words and then look directly at him. "It never occurred to me that you didn't see the note."

He stares back at me, silent, for several long minutes. "But the baby. How could you not tell me about the baby? How could you keep that from me? From my family?"

My head rocks back and forth as I say the words, knowing they sound trite and wrong now that I know he didn't choose this. "I was so hurt when you didn't come. At first, I just went to Auntie Wendy's to wait for you, thinking it would be a day or two. Maybe a week. But you never came. I thought you gave up on me. On us. Why would you want our baby if you didn't even want me?"

"Oh, Sydney." He looks up at the ceiling, his lips closed tightly, and I wonder if he's praying for strength, or to God for help, but then see tears sliding down his face. My heart breaks for the millionth time tonight as I witness his pain and know that I did this to him. I reach for his hand, but when I touch him, he shakes me away and then drags it down his face, wiping away the tears. "So, what do you want from me? Why did you come? Why now?"

"Isn't it obvious, Justin?" I look down at my frail form, at the body I don't even recognize anymore, and then back at him. "I don't have a lot of time left. I need to decide what to do with Justine. I can leave her to Kelly if you don't want her."

His eyes blaze a dark blue as he whips his gaze to mine. "The hell you will! She's my daughter, even if I've never had the chance to be her father. You aren't going to keep that right from me anymore."

I nod, not able to argue with him because I know now that what I've done has cost us all. "Justin, I wouldn't be here if I didn't want the same thing. I just—I thought—well, it doesn't matter what I thought anymore. I was wrong. You can see her anytime you want."

I lean over and slide the notebook toward me, grabbing a loose pen that's sitting on the table. I turn the page, signifying so much with one flip of the paper, burying the note, and write down my address in Florida for him.

Now that I've said everything I can, I stand. I'm exhausted and weak and feel like I'm about to collapse. He lifts his gaze from the notebook to me, a look of concern sweeping quickly across his features. "I need to go." I point to the address I've left for him. "That's where you can find us."

"You're leaving?" His voice is finally soft again.

I nod. Honestly, I don't want to go. I want him to take me in his arms and tell me he forgives me and that he never stopped loving me. I want him to make me feel so good that I forget I'm dying, that I'm never going to see my little girl grow up, and that I'm never going to know what it feels like to have forever with someone. I just can't for one more second, though. One more second and I'm going to break apart at the seams that I've barely been holding together for so, so long.

Instead, I move and place a dry kiss on his cheek. I inhale deeply when I do, savoring his heat and the smell of him and the whiskey on his breath, and I whisper one more time, "I'm sorry. I'm so sorry, Justin."

He doesn't stop me when I walk away, when I turn the handle of the door, when I walk through, or when I stand out in the hallway. Every single thing I held on to for the last four years, I leave behind as the door slams shut.

LOVE NOTES

CHAPTER TWENTY-TWO

I stare out the window of the plane and look down at the blue-green water rolling in waves across the ocean as we start our descent into Tampa. It's been five days since Sydney came to see me. Five days that I've had to rethink every emotion I've had over the last four years concerning her. Five days to think about a daughter I didn't know I had. Five days to try to accept that the only woman I've ever loved is dying.

The last two days, I spent with my family back on the farm, telling them everything, letting them share in my shock, my happiness, and my grief. Like me, they were angry to learn they had missed three years of the life of their granddaughter, and Jonathan his niece, but also like me, are grateful for the time that lay ahead with her. When they learned how sick Sydney is, any feelings of anger at her were pushed aside by bigger feelings of the loss we knew we would all soon struggle with.

I spent hours talking with my mom about what it meant to be a mother, a parent, trying to understand the path and choice that lay before me now. I feel like Sydney and I failed each other in so many ways, ways that could have been avoided, and I am determined to not fail my daughter. I sat in the cottage for hours, remembering every moment we spent there laughing, talking, and loving each other.

I took the ATV and went to the pond where I asked her to move to Brooklyn with me. I sat there until the sun set and stars began twinkling in the sky, wondering if I should have done things differently. What if I had listened to my head and waited until I had moved to Brooklyn, found out what my life would be like first before asking her to move there, instead of acting on instinct and my heart? What could the last four years of my life, or her life, of our life together have been like? It's four more years that I may have possibly gotten to spend with her. Four more years I'll never get back, and three years of my daughter's life that I've missed.

The anger I felt at learning so much from her the other night pales in comparison to the sadness I feel over the time we've wasted. Now, more than ever, knowing how fragile and unpredictable this life is, I know I can't waste another second. I'm not sure what's going to happen after I knock on her door, but I do know that I'm going to do every single thing in my power to make the time she has left, the time we have left, happy.

When the plane finally bounces on the runway, and the attendants announce that our seatbelts can safely be unbuckled, I pounce from my first-class seat, grab my guitar from the overhead, and then stride through the jetway as soon as the door to the airplane is open. I walk directly to the rental car counter, arrange for a car, and then grab my bag as it circles around the carousel.

I walk outside and stagger against the assault of the August heat and humidity. I find the shuttle for the rental car garage and hop on. Once I secure the car, I punch her address into the GPS and smile when I see I only have another hour in front of me until I'm there. Traffic is light, and I'm thrilled when I pull down her street and find the house with her number on the front. I park the car, leave my stuff inside, and step out. I smile as I look at her home. It's nestled on the corner of a dead-end street, and I can see the ocean beyond the bushes lining her yard.

I stroll up the front walk and ring the bell, my nerves zinging at the anticipation of seeing her again. There's a car in the driveway, so I assume she's home, but no one has come to the door. I try the handle but find it locked, and I frown. I scratch the scruff on my chin and move off the path, circling around the house to the back. As the beach comes into view, I see people scattered about and sweep my gaze across the landscape, stopping when I find two blondes sitting at the edge of the water, playing in the sand.

I recognize Sydney immediately, knowing that must be Justine with her, and marvel at how much bigger she is than when I originally held her in my arms. I stop where the grassy edge of her lawn meets the sand and toe my sneakers off before making my way across the beach, my eyes never leaving them. I'm about six feet away when Sydney's head turns in my direction and I watch her expression change to one of surprise. By the time she's standing, I'm at her side, unable to break the gaze I have locked on both of them.

"You're here." Her bottom lip is between her teeth, and my insides warm at the sight, happy to know that some things haven't changed.

"I'm here." I lean forward and kiss her tenderly on the cheek, her eyes closing softly as I do. "You look beautiful."

Her eyes open slowly, and I'm relieved to see a smile break across her face. "Do you want to meet your daughter?"

I look down at the doll-like figure still playing with clumps of sand at her mother's feet and take in her soft wavy locks, the same exact color of her mother's, nodding my head eagerly. Syd kneels to her level and puts a sandy finger under Justine's chin to bring her attention to her instead of the mud. "Hey, I have someone I want you to meet, okay?"

"Okay, Momma." The little girl pops up from the sand on her stubby legs and looks up at me, her hand moving to shield her eyes from the bright sun shining behind me. I blink when the blue of her eyes meets mine, noting their color is the exact same as mine, and wonder how in the world I didn't notice when I held her in my arms two years ago. Her face scrunches up as she looks at me and then turns and looks back over at her mom. "Is that Daddy?"

My heart stutters in my chest at hearing her, and I look over at Syd, my brows raised. She raises her finger up in a gesture to Tini to wait a minute and then quietly says, "I'll explain after, okay?"

I nod my head, still in the clouds at hearing this sweet girl calling me Daddy. She turns her attention back to Justine and nods. "Yes, this is your daddy, sweetie. He's finally home from work."

I give her a puzzled look, and she whispers for me to just roll with it and promises to explain after. I feel a sandy hand slide into mine and look down to find Justine standing next to me. "You want to build a castle with me?" It sounds more like, 'you wanna buwd a cawtle wid me', and I beam at the invitation. Nodding, I tell her, "Absolutely." I swear, my heart triples in size when her little hand grips tighter and pulls me down to sit in the sand beside her.

If anyone ever wants to question whether or not love at first sight exists, I can attest that it does. I know instantly that I'm not going to want to miss another second of her young life and have never felt more at peace than I do at this moment, with wet sand running through my fingers and my daughter's giggles lifting into the wind. The sound is sweeter than any melody that has ever been written.

Sydney sits in the sand next to me and watches us play, a content smile on her face, and then looks over at me. "How long are you staying?"

I shrug and smile over at her hopefully. "As long as you let me."

As I sit in the sand, the hot Florida sunshine warming my face, watching Justin play with our daughter, I know that, even though I've made a hundred bad decisions, going to him and telling him about her was definitely the best one I've ever made. The look of pure joy and love on his face when she placed her hand in his will be ingrained in my soul for whatever time I have left.

The heat of the sun is wearing me down so I stand, brush the sand from my legs, and announce it's time to go in. After a few moans of protest from Tini, we make our way back across the beach, pails in hand, and onto the back lawn of our yard. I smile when I see Justin scoop up his shoes, an action in itself that seems small but, to me, demonstrates his ease at being here already.

I lead him across the lawn, Tini's hand grasped firmly in his, open the sliding glass door to the kitchen, and step through. The cool air of the house dances over my skin, bringing instant relief from the heat outside. Justin slides the glass closed after we're all through and groans out loud. "Oh my God, the air conditioning feels good!"

I smile, agreeing one hundred percent, but also because I can't believe he's actually standing in my kitchen with us right now. "You want something to drink?"

He chuckles and looks up at me sheepishly. "Ice water?" We both grin widely and then break into laughter, Tini looking back and forth at each of us, trying to figure out what's so funny. I take two glasses and a sippy cup from the cupboard, then turn to find Justin, his hands taking the glasses from mine.

I watch as he moves to the refrigerator to fill them, but he stops mid-stride a few feet from its reach. He turns back around, a confused look on his face, and then points to the rectangle paper that's stuck to its front under a magnet. "You didn't cash it?"

I shake my head. "Not yet."

He looks at me and frowns. "Why?"

I shrug. "I haven't needed it yet. I make a pretty good living off my books. I've published seven in the last four years, and I just sold the screen rights to the second one."

"Then put it in an account for Justine. It's half a million dollars, Syd. You can't leave it stuck to the fridge."

I nod. "Okay, if that's what you want." I frown. "Actually, I don't think it's even good anymore. I think a check is only good for six months or so."

"Then I'll write you a new one, with the interest added, since that means it's been sitting in my account for the last two years." He plucks it off the fridge and shakes his head. "My accountant should have told me about this."

"I still wouldn't have cashed it," I state, just to let him know it wouldn't have mattered either way.

He smirks and begins filling the glasses. "Still stubborn as always, I see?"

"Mommy, I have sand in my bum!" Tini's little voice wails between us, as she wiggles around.

"Okay, my little peanut. Let's get you in the tub." Justin trades a glass of water with me for the sippy cup, fills it quickly, and then hands it to Tini. "Let me just give Daddy a quick tour, okay?"

"My room! Let's show him my room!" She bounces up and down, sand sifting from her bottom on the tile floor as she does, then grabs his hand. "Come on!"

The way his face lights up when she grasps his fingers with hers sends a surge of happiness through me that I haven't felt in years. In my heart, I knew, I really knew that Justin would come for Justine, but seeing them together gives me a renewed sense of hope that everything will be okay for her. Even without me. I follow them down the hall into her bedroom, pointing out the living room and bathroom as I go, and stand in the doorway of her room as she shows him around.

She's chattering away, introducing each and every stuffed fox that's sitting on her bed, his face a mix of emotions when he turns to me, his brows raised. "Foxes?"

I shrug and give him a soft smile. "I have a thing for foxes. Now, she does, too."

"And, Daddy, look at my farm! Mommy said you have a farm!" I watch her pull him down to the floor, pull the big plastic barn apart to open it, and then start showing him all the animals that live inside. He turns his head to me, surprise and gratitude shining from his eyes as he quietly says thank you. Even though he wasn't here physically, I made sure Tini knew everything about him, about us, and tried to bring pieces of that into her life in any way I could find.

I watch him interact with our daughter for a few more minutes. As he notices the frame on the nightstand next to her bed, he moves to pick it up in his hands. It's a picture of Justin and me, his arm wrapped tightly around me, both of us laughing at a cook-out we went to at Adam's. Kelly had taken it that summer and surprised me with it as a gift to me at her wedding, telling me that Justin and I were next. He turns to me, the frame still in his hand, his lids blinking rapidly as he holds it up to me and smiles. "I've never seen this."

"Kelly gave it to me."

His brows lift and his head cocks in surprise. "Huh." Then he sets it back down and turns his attention back to his daughter. "Did Mommy ever tell you the story about the time we named a cow after her?"

Tini giggles wildly. "Mommy's not a cow!"

He joins in her laughter and tells her the story about the first time I ever went to the farm. My throat clenches, and I feel tears starting to form, so I turn away to let them share this moment together, and go fill the tub. When it's ready, I break up their little farm party, stripping her out of her bathing suit, and plop her into the warm water.

Justin seems content to just sit and watch our routine from the closed toilet seat, a smile always present on his face. When we're done, I dry her off, spread lotion all over her warm, soft skin, and slide a nightgown over her. She walks to one of the bathroom drawers and takes out a pull-up, putting it on herself and declaring she's a big girl to Justin.

We laugh and share in her excitement, both of us understanding that the simple joy of raising our daughter carries so much weight for both of us. Me, trying to cherish every single day, every single moment I have left with her. Him, learning and discovering what a lifetime ahead with her will be.

CHAPTER TWENTY-THREE

I ingest every single morsel of laughter, touch, and word we share throughout the afternoon, storing it away to treasure later. Sydney makes grilled cheese sandwiches and chicken noodle soup for dinner, most of which I can't help but notice she barely eats. I'm surprised by how independent Justine is; feeding herself the soup with her small, plastic spoon, and then helping her mom by carrying her little bowl over to the counter when she's finished.

Sydney has done an incredible job of raising her. Knowing this is like a double-edged sword, though. On one hand, I'm so grateful to her for instilling so much love and warmth to create this perfect little being, but on the other, I'm angry that I didn't get to be a part of that. And, again, my heart is overrun with the joy I feel at knowing I have the rest of my life to watch her grow and see who she becomes, and then breaks when I remember that soon, I'll be doing it alone.

I just finished reading Brown Bear to her for the third time and now sit transfixed as I watch little puffs of breath escape from her lips as she sleeps. She reminds me so much of Sydney. They breathe exactly the same way. I reach up and trail my fingers softly over her silky locks, the light coconut scent of her shampoo lifting into the air as I do. I can't believe she's mine, that we made something so entirely perfect. It still doesn't seem real to me.

"Hey." Sydney's soft voice behind me has me turning around to the door. "You okay in here?"

I nod, place the little cardboard book on the nightstand, and then rise and leave the room. Sydney pulls the door quietly closed behind me and then turns back down the hall and moves into the living room. She sits on the couch and pats the cushion next to her, inviting me to do the same. "Guess we should talk, huh?"

We haven't had one moment alone without Justine by our side since I arrived, so even though the afternoon was every single thing I could have hoped for, we've said nothing of any real substance. "I guess so." I give her a small smile and sit on the offered seat.

"I'm really glad you came, Justin."

"Did you think I wouldn't?" I question, hoping after everything that happened last week, she really knows I wouldn't have made any other choice.

"I knew you would. I just didn't know when." She wrings her hands in her lap. "You were so mad."

I grimace as I think about our last meeting. "I was, but I'm not anymore. We've wasted enough time." I look at her, really look at her, and for the first time notice just how tired and frail she is. "Are you okay?"

"Today's a good day." She brushes her hand through her short locks and looks back over at me, one side of her mouth pulling down in a small frown. "There are still more good than bad so far."

"How long do they say, Syd?" I shift my eyes away, afraid to look at her, and ask again to be clear. "How much more time?"

I feel her raise her shoulders, lower them, and sigh. "They never give you an exact number. You know, like, I'm going to hold it against them if they get it wrong. But they guess four months, maybe six."

My eyes fly to hers in shock, and I echo her response, disbelief ringing in my voice, my heart dropping into my stomach. "Four months? Sydney, that's not long enough." I shift on the couch so I can move a little closer and take one of her hands in mine. I'm surprised to feel how cool and paper thin her skin feels. "What can I do?"

She squeezes her hand in mine. "You're doing it."

"That's easy. But what else? What else can I do? What can we do?"

Her short hair swishes back and forth as she shakes her head. "Just love her, Justin. Love her enough for both of us when I'm gone."

I rake my hand through my hair roughly and lower my gaze to meet hers. "I'll love her the only way I know how, Syd, and that's with my whole heart."

She nods her head, biting her lip, blinking quickly at the tears beginning to fall. I pull her into my arms then and hold her, trying to offer what comfort I can with the simple gesture. I fight back my own tears as I do, promising myself that, no matter what, I will be strong enough for both of us. She feels so small in my arms, like a baby bird, her bones so close to the surface of her skin, and I pull her in a little closer to try to make her warm.

After some time, we pull apart and sit quietly for a minute. I look around the living room and notice for the first time that there are candid photographs lining every wall. There's an entire wall filled with pictures of Tini, from infancy until now, and I stand and walk over so I can get a closer look. I run my fingers over the photos as I move along the wall.

The other wall contains pictures of her dad, Kelly, Adam, Kelly's mom, times at the bar, and yes, even pictures of me. I stop and look at one and study it. I'm sitting on a stool at Hook's, my guitar sitting upright in my lap, the neck covering most of my face as I stare back at the camera. I look angry, but I know I'm not. I remember Sydney taking that picture of me. She was trying to get a picture of me so she could make a poster to hang around town about my gigs there on Saturdays, and she told me to be more serious. She was laughing behind the camera, making it almost impossible for me to keep a straight face.

Memories of us, of her life, of everyone she loves cover her walls as a reminder. I frown and wonder how hard that must be for her, knowing what she knows. Seeing the pictures of Tini reminds me that she never explained how my little girl knew I was her father, but now I might understand. "Is this how Justine knew I was her father?"

I point to the pictures on the wall and then move to sit back down next to her, watching as she lifts her head up and down. "Uh-huh. But she wanted to know why her daddy wasn't here like her other friends' daddies, so I told her you were at work." She slaps her hand over her face at the admission and groans. "It sounds so dumb, right? But what do you tell a three-year-old when you don't even know the answer?"

I laugh. "Honey, I'm home!" I spit out, trying to make light of the situation. I know I can't change the choices we made in the past, but I can choose now to try to make the best of our future.

"So, I guess I need to go check into a hotel. It's getting late and you look tired." I move to rise but falter when I see the stricken look on her face.

"You're leaving?"

I settle back down and nod. "Well, yeah, but I'll be back in the morning." Did she really think I was leaving already?

"You don't have to go, Justin. You can stay here." It comes out soft and unsure.

My heart jumps in my chest at her invitation. "Are you sure? I don't want to push too much too fast."

"I'm sure." She stands. "I have a guest room. You can stay."

"Okay, I'd really like that." I rise and tell her I need to go get my things from my car if I'm staying. She waits by the door as I gather my things and then shows me to a room, one door down from Tini's, decorated in a pretty beach theme.

"Kelly comes to visit a lot. She would have killed me if I made her sleep on the couch, so a three-bedroom house it was." She shrugs, knowing that's all the explanation needed on the subject. She points to a door at the very end of the hall. "That's my room. Just let me know if you need anything, okay?"

I really want to stay up all night and talk to her. Ask her questions about what it was like when she was pregnant, if the delivery was hard, and if Tini was a good baby. I want to know when she got her first tooth, said her first word, and took her first step. And Sydney, has she dated anyone since me? Does she still throw random quotes out at strangers, and how does she sleep at night? I'd ask her about her books, but I've bought and read every one. There's a lot of downtime on the road, and it was a way for me to feel closer to her.

But, instead, I watch her walk down the hall, grace me with a small smile and wave before closing the bedroom door behind her, and I just feel thankful that I still have time to learn everything.

I STRIP OUT THE CLOTHES I'VE BEEN WEARING SINCE THIS afternoon on the beach and then step into my shower, grateful to finally rinse the sand still sticking to my body in places. I think about the fact that Justin is here, in this house, twenty feet down the hall, and sigh, relief pouring over me that he stayed. I don't care if it's selfish, but now that he's finally here, now that he finally knows about Tini and about me, I don't want him to go.

I've missed him. I've missed him every day for as long as I can remember. I shake away my conscience when it starts to niggle its way in, trying to remind me that it's my own fault that he wasn't here for the last four years and push it away. I promised myself that I wasn't going to dwell on the mistakes I've made and just focus on today; the here and now.

I finish rinsing off, step out of the shower, dry off, and patter into my bedroom. I take my night shirt from the hook in my closet and slide it over my body, the material worn and soft with age, and then slip a pair of panties on. I pull back the covers on my large, king-size bed and slide between the cool cotton sheets. It's early, just after nine, but these days, I go to bed early, trying to get as much rest as I can, hoping to keep my energy levels up.

Instead of falling asleep, I toss and turn, flip this way and that, throw the covers off and then pull them back on. After an hour, I lay flat on my back and watch the ceiling fan moving in a slow, lazy circle overhead, my mind doing the same. I think about the fact again that Justin is a mere twenty feet away. I literally ache to feel his arms around me again, to feel the comfort and safety of being in them as I fall asleep. It's been four years since I've felt him against me.

Screw it. You only live once, and damn it, in my case, not very much longer. I throw back the covers, slide out of bed, open my door, and creep softly down the hallway until I'm in front of his closed door. I raise my hand three times before I finally work up the courage to knock lightly.

When the door slowly swings open, a bare-chested Justin now standing in front of me, concern on his face, I take a shy step back. "You okay, Syd?"

I nod, chewing on my lip, trying to figure out how to ask him what I want. He takes a step further out into the hallway and, frowning, raises a hand and pulls my lip tenderly from my grasp. "What's wrong?"

"Nothing." I shuffle my feet back and forth. "I mean, I can't sleep." I look up at him, my heart hammering against my chest.

He lets out a long sigh. "Me neither." His hand lifts and his fingers brush through his locks, leaving them a sexy, tousled mess, and gives me a crooked grin. "You think I'd be used to sleeping in new places by now."

"Will you sleep with me?" I blurt it out, my face heating beneath my cheeks, as I watch his eyes pop open. "I mean, you know, sleep with me? Not have sex with me. Just sleep." I stammer the rest.

His crooked grin blooms into a full-blown smile, his eyes crinkling more around the corners than I remember. "Really?" He turns and shuts his bedroom door. "You have no idea how much I'd like that."

"Really?" I breath out in surprised relief.

"Syd, I miss you. So damn much." The smile is gone, and instead, a sadness sweeps across his features.

"I miss you, too." I turn and then look at him over my shoulder. "Come on."

CHAPTER TWENTY-FOUR

I follow behind into her room and then watch as she shuts the door softly after her. I know she said she just wants me to sleep with her, but it's hard to try to explain that to the area below my waist line, which is stirring as I think about sliding into the bed with her. She spins around and sweeps her hands out around her. "This is my room."

Instead of looking around, I squint my eyes and take a step closer to her, my eyes taking in what she's wearing. I admire her long, bare legs before moving my line of sight to the bottom hem of her shirt, up past her chest, finally meeting her curious ones. "Is that my shirt?"

Her brows shoot up before her head dips down to look at the article of clothing that fits her more like a dress. It's faded to a light blue, much lighter than the blue denim color it was the afternoon I gave it to her to wear at the cottage so long ago, after we were caught in the rain storm. Her hands fidget with the buttons as she looks back up at me and raises her shoulders. "I love this shirt."

"I love seeing you in my shirt," I say, my voice growing gravely.

"Cliché much?" she retorts, laughing lightly.

I take the five steps separating us and stand inches away, looking down into her eyes as she raises them to meet mine. I know this is wrong. I know it's too soon. But I also know we don't have enough time, and I want to make the most of every minute we have left after wasting so many. I cup her face gently in my hands. "I really want to kiss you right now, but…"

Her lips curve upward, her eyes growing a little watery as she murmurs her reply. "But?"

"But I'm so afraid I'm going to hurt you." This isn't what I said to her the first time, but so much has changed, and I truly am afraid to break her. She's so tiny and so fragile.

"There's nothing left to break." Her lips form a straight line as she steps back out of my touch and begins unbuttoning the shirt. "There's hardly anything left of me ‚Justin." A small tear trickles down her cheek, and I take a step forward when I see her hands trembling. She shakes her head no and I stop. "I'm not the same anymore." She pulls the shirt apart and opens it wide so I can see what her body has become.

I can't help the gasp that escapes, and scowl at myself when I see her flinch in response. She told me she had several operations, but I didn't comprehend what that meant for her physically. Her body is skeleton thin, and scars line most of her torso. She yanks the shirt closed and clenches her eyes tightly. "I'm sorry. I know it's ugly to look at!"

I go to her and pull her face back into my hands. "Open your eyes, Syd." She scrunches them up more tightly and grimaces. I shake her very lightly. "Open them." Her lids slowly open, and her eyes snap to mine. "You're not ugly, Sydney. You could never be ugly. I was surprised. I'm so stupid, and I didn't know."

Tears are trickling from the corners of her eyes, and I lean down to kiss them away. I follow their tracks down her cheeks and then move across until I find her lips and finally, finally seal them over hers. She moans and releases the grip she has on the shirt to bring her arms around my neck, her hands gripping my nape. I slide my hands so one is behind her small back and the other at the opening of her shirt, trailing my hand softly down the front of her body. I can feel the bumps of her scars as I go, and feel her muscles clench, then move to whisper in her ear. "You're beautiful, Sydney, so Goddamn beautiful."

I hear her gasp out a small sob, her hands moving to clutch my hair as I move my mouth to her neck and slowly down her chest. I slide the shirt off her arms and move to my knees, placing a kiss over every single scar, trying to show I love every piece of her. When I'm done, I rise and lift her, scooping her in my arms, her head falling on my shoulder, her arms wrapping tightly around me, as I carry her to the bed.

Tenderly, I lay her down and then slide my boxers off before climbing beside her. I take her shaky hand and move it to lay on my chest. "You can touch me, Syd. Touch me anywhere you want." And she does. She lays her hand flat and runs it over my stomach, my abdomen still tight from all the hours I've spent on stage, and then uses her fingers to graze over the hair settled in the groove of my pelvis, until her hand wraps around my cock and begins stroking it softly.

I want this to be about her, but feeling her hand on me causes a surge of desire for her that causes my length to throb and jerk in her hand. I lean down and capture her lips in mine, my tongue pushing against her mouth until it opens so I can taste her. She pushes back against me, turning the kiss into something hard and needy, shifting her body so it's pressed up against mine.

Snaking a hand around her tiny waist, I pull her flush to me, my mouth opening in a low moan when my cock rubs against her core. She rolls to her back, grabbing onto my arm as she goes, taking me with her, splaying her legs wide so I can fit inside. I move between them, my lips locked with hers again, until I feel her hand grip my cock again and rub it against her clit, eliciting another moan from me.

"I want this to last, Sydney, but you're killing me here." I pant into her ear, then still when I realize my choice of words.

She chuckles, vibrating under me, and turns her head so her eyes can look into mine. "Then die with me." And then she thrusts her hips up until my cock slides into her entrance. As soon as I feel her walls clench around me, I surge forward, meeting her hips, fusing us together, both of us losing ourselves in the ecstasy of our love.

When we're done, she lays across my chest, but unlike before, her hair no longer trails in streams across, tickling my skin. Instead, I brush my fingers through her short locks, wondering at the silky likeness to Tini's hair.

"Are you okay?" I'm so worried about hurting her.

"I'm absolutely perfect," she purrs from my chest.

"Just for the record, I hope you know I'll be *sleeping* with you every night from now on."

She giggles and then softly asks, "Will you do something else for me, Justin?"

"Anything." There's absolutely no hesitation in my response because I will literally do anything I can if it will make her happy.

"Would you marry me?" My hands still in her hair, my heart skipping a beat. "Will you make me and Justine yours?"

I sit up, pushing her with me, and look into her eyes, tears gathering in the corners of mine. "Oh, Sydney, don't you know that you already are?"

MY BARE FEET SQUISH INTO THE COOL, MOSSY GRASS AS I WALK over the crest of the short hill, and I beam as I take in the sight spread out in front of me. Standing beside the pond where I know our daughter was created, is Justin. He's at the top of a path that's been outlined in yellow rose petals being scattered by Justine as she walks several feet in front of me. He's wearing a dark blue suit that magnifies the color of his eyes. To his right stands Jonathan, as his best man, and to his left, Kelly, dressed in a beautiful gray silk dress, as my matron of honor. Chairs have been set up in two small rows but only contain our immediate family, which, of course, includes Kelly's.

When Justin agreed to marry me, my only request was that we have it here, on the farm, and I couldn't think of a more beautiful place than this. Kelly, Shannon, and Pam worked liked bees to make all the arrangements, pulling everything together in three short weeks, knowing every day matters to us right now.

Justin hired a private plane to fly us here last week, not wanting to expose me to any germs flying public may have risked. Justine declared that it was the only way she wanted to travel from that day forward, and I suspect, if she truly demands it, Justin will give it to her. They have bonded so much more quickly and deeply than I could have wished for, and that alone brings me so much peace.

Because time was so short, and finding a wedding dress in that timeframe unlikely, I am wearing Kelly's. Her mom altered it to fit my thin frame, and as the soft organza fabric floats over my legs as I make my way down the aisle, I know it was the absolute perfect choice.

I finally come to a stop beside Justin, my dad giving my hand a final squeeze before he kisses me softly on the cheek and whispers he loves me. I turn, slipping my hands into Justin's, and we say the simple vows we requested the justice of the peace marry us with. He slides a diamond laced band over my ring finger, and I, a solid gray platinum band over his, then we crash into each other's arms when it's announced the groom may kiss his bride, cheers rising up around us.

After the wedding, we climb into golf carts Justin rented and make the short drive back to the house. We're having the reception at Hook's, as we both agreed no other place would do. When we arrive, it's to a bar full of all our regulars, waiting with open arms to welcome and congratulate us. They've decorated the bar with enough white silk and flowers to possibly cover three restaurants, but we revel in the joy of the day and drink in every moment.

Shannon wheels a huge wedding cake out from the back room, and we engage in the traditional cutting of the cake and, of course, shoving it into each other's mouths playfully. Justin plants more kisses on me throughout the day then I can count, and I savor each and every one. Tini is on the dance floor, being twirled around by Jonathan, her laughter filling the room, and I smile, knowing that no matter what, her life will always be filled with love.

Halfway through the celebration, the crowd talks Justin into singing a few songs. After someone runs home and grabs his guitar and an amp, he sits on a stool at the front of the room and plays for us. What makes the performance so magical is that he doesn't sing one song he's released since becoming famous. He only sings his old stuff, the songs that we always used to request from him. We sing along with him, his face beaming with happiness. Tini moves to stand next to him, until someone plops a stool down beside Justin, which she climbs up on. He shares the mic with her, and the crowd gasps in surprise when they hear her beautiful voice.

In the middle of his performance, he asks everyone to settle down for a moment, then gazes around the room at everyone when we do. A content smile is on his face as he begins to speak. "I played a lot of small pubs, fairs, and events before I played all those Saturday nights here a few years ago." He strums his fingers across the strings of the guitar softly and continues. "But, honestly, nothing ever came close to how I felt about playing here for all of you. You became family to me. So, I wrote this one for all of you." His smile grows wider when we all collectively start murmuring our surprise. "And I know I played on Saturdays, but the song is called Fridays, 'cause it just worked better, so you'll have to cut me a little slack on that one."

He gives the room one more sweep and then starts playing the song for us.

"Waste my time, walking down a street I don't know in Boston
Can't make up my mind, decisions are changing things mask taping
It's fine tossin' and turning 'til the sun comes up
No I don't mind, you can get in my bed just don't get in my head

I said a couple things, I got louder
Told me a few things, I got problems

making a fool out of myself, and it piles damn it piles
I hope streets will fill when I'm done, banners on the wall
And I'm coming down entertain my lungs
Face I'm feeling fine slowly hear me mine

Open my eyes head off the pillow I see blue
Go ahead and cry about your parent one more time
Always supportive, but no one supports shit when you gotta make dues
Out on your porch and thinking the mine of accusation

Fridays don't feel like Fridays anymore
Maybe it's 'cause I look forward

*Of making a fool out of myself, and it piles damn it piles
I hope streets will fill when I'm done banners on the wall
And I'm coming down entertain my lungs
Face I'm feeling fine, slowly hear me mine."*

IT'S BEAUTIFUL, AND EVEN THOUGH MOST OF THE WORDS ONLY make sense to me, every person in the room breaks into wild applause when he's done. Except for me. I sit and stare until his gaze finds me, and I simply mouth, "I love you."

Several hours later, the guests have left, and only Kelly, Adam, Jonathan, Justin, and I remain. Pam and Tom took Tini home with them so we could have a few hours to ourselves. I'm so tired, but I don't want the day to end, so we sit, and we talk, and we laugh. Today was a really good day, but each day has been getting harder for me; the pain is starting to get worse, my body beginning to weaken.

Justin looks over at me knowingly and suggests it's time to call it a night. I nod, grateful that he always seems to know what I need. I rise from the table, but Kelly jumps up and tells me to stay. She digs around in her purse, pulls out a dollar, and walks over to the jukebox. I smile and laugh, knowing what's coming. I watch her punch in some numbers and then scoot her way over to me.

I stand and get ready to croon out our favorite song, one more time, and then still when I hear violins instead and swing my gaze to her in surprise.

"You never had your first dance," she states quietly. She leans over and kisses my cheek and then sits back down. I look over at Justin, who's already standing, and we walk together to the center of the dance floor. His arms wrap around me, like they've done so many times before, but this time, it's as husband and wife, and we start swaying to our song, the very first song we ever danced to.

His breath is warm against my ear as he whispers against it. "Have I ever told you I love you?"

I bite my lip, trying to keep my tears at bay, and shake my head against his. "You do?"

He pulls me tighter and kisses my cheek. "I do."

I smile, knowing I'll never say truer words when I reply. "Good, 'cause I love you, too."

CHAPTER TWENTY-FIVE

SIX MONTHS LATER

We buried Sydney three weeks ago, under an old Oak tree on the far side of the field overlooking our pond. Per her request, we didn't have a big funeral; only her dad, Kelly's family, and my family were present. For her burial, it was only me. I placed her in the ground, in a stone-gray casket lined in white silk, with her dressed only in my old blue shirt. She made me promise, telling me it was the only thing she could ever sleep comfortably in.

After the wedding, we went back to Florida and spent her good days filled with making memories together. We took Tini to Disney World, me insisting Sydney wear a surgical mask over her face at all times to keep from getting sick, and her trying to take it off every chance I wasn't looking. We sailed to the Bahamas on a yacht I rented so she and Tini could swim with the dolphins on Paradise Island. I booked a private plane and flew us to a cabin in Vermont for New Year's so we could watch Tini play in the snow.

There were quiet days as well, when she got too weak to travel anymore, so we sat on the beach with the sun on our faces and took joy in Tini jumping in the waves, bringing us pink shells she found buried in the sand. Each time, she would try to fly with the seagulls lining the shore, her laughter carrying on the wind.

And then there was the worst day. The day she fought to take one more breath as I held her in my arms, Tini wrapped in hers, my heart shattering into a million pieces when the last puff of air passed through her lips. Tini shaking her mother, begging her to wake up as I tried to keep myself from breaking in half while I pulled her from her mother's arms.

I try not to focus on that memory, instead forcing myself to remember Syd's laughter, her warm lips on mine, and the look in her eyes when she watched her daughter play. But it's still a struggle for me. I'm so angry that she's gone and that our time together was so short.

I walk up to the mound of dirt under the tree that's just starting to show new sprouts of grass poking through and sit down beside her. Mom must have come earlier today because there are fresh tulips planted at the top of the grave. I didn't put up a headstone, and instead, just carved her name into the Oak tree. She said she just wanted to be up here with nature, to run free and still feel her toes in the grass.

I've come every day since I laid her here, but I'm leaving tomorrow to go back to Florida and pack up her house. I've put it off as long as I can, and know I need to do it before I head back to the studio to record next month.

It's time for me to go back to work. The label has been great about all the time I've taken off, and I know they would let me take more if I wanted, but honestly, I've got so many emotions pent up inside of me, it will be good to write some of them down and get them out there. Kelly helped me to hire a really good nanny that I'm taking to L.A. with me and Tini.

The label and the studio have worked out a great schedule with me, setting up ground rules around the hours I'm available to work and dates I can tour. I think they're just so damn happy I'm coming back that they would have agreed to anything I proposed. We'll be in California for three months to record, then I'll tour for three months this summer to support the new album, and then I'll come back to the farm for six months with Tini.

It works for now. She's not in school. I'll have to figure things out when she gets a little older. I explain all this out loud to Sydney as I sit by her grave and hope she'd be happy with the decisions I've made. I really want to do what's right for our daughter, and I think this is it.

I lay back in the grass, wanting to feel closer to her, and turn on my side to face the mound. "I miss you so much, Sydney. I can't sleep at night. I pace around the cottage and watch Tini sleep instead. Do you know she breaths just like you when she's sleeping?" I laugh softly to myself. "Of course, you wouldn't know that. You can't watch yourself sleep."

I listen to the birds chirp around me and just lay on the ground next to her, thinking about what else I need to make sure she knows before I leave tomorrow. "Oh, I need to figure out what to do for Tini's birthday. You didn't tell me what to do. I can't believe she's going to be four in a couple weeks. She said she wants to go to Brazil because that's where Dora the Explorer lives, and she wants to help her catch the fox." I laugh at the memory of Tini sharing this request with me yesterday. "I mean, really, Syd? How does she even know about Brazil?"

Sitting back up, I rest my hands on my bent knees. "Don't worry, though. I'm not taking her to Brazil. Maybe to Hawaii instead? I mean, we'll be in L.A. anyway. That's probably too much, huh?"

Shaking my head, I ask her one last question before I go. "Have I ever told you that I love you?"

I keep waiting for an answer, even though I know I'm not going to get one, and rest my head wearily on top of my hands, unable to stop the tears that have started falling from my eyes again. I honestly don't know how I have any left to cry, but they keep coming. My body shakes when I think about walking away from this spot, from her, knowing I won't be back for a while.

I raise my head to the heavens and scream at God for taking her from me. "Why? Why did you take her? You should have taken me! I can't do this without her! I don't want to live without her here! Why, God? Why?" Tears are running in rivers down my face, blinding me, as I drop my head onto my knees and sob uncontrollably, and repeat again and again, "How can I do this without you, Syndey?"

I'm not sure how long I've cried. I can feel the shadows growing longer around me and know I need to leave, but I can't bring myself to move from this spot. I hear a rustling sound and lift my head, curious to see who might have come, thinking maybe Kelly, and freeze.

A small red fox sits at the foot of Syd's grave, it's little paws resting in the fresh dirt, staring back at me. I stare back, waiting to see what it does, but it just sits there, not moving at all. I begin to wonder if I'm dreaming, so I speak to it. "Hey there, little one."

It finally moves, taking two tiny steps in my direction, and then stops again. I smile, surprised it's getting so close to me, and then frown for a minute, surprised it doesn't seem to be afraid.

The fox takes a couple more steps toward me and stops again, still staring at me. I look at it, and the strangest feeling spreads over me. For the first time in weeks, I feel like a weight has been lifted off my chest. A sense of peace settles within my soul. I cock my head, staring at the fox intently, and wonder if what I'm about to do is crazy.

"Sydney?" It comes as a whisper. I'm not sure if I believe I'm even asking the fox this question, or maybe I'm not. Maybe I'm asking God.

The fox tilts it's head and runs in a small circle on the small hill before hopping lightly back onto the mossy grass. I watch as it kneads its front paws into the ground and then looks up at me.

Knowing this is absolutely crazy, I ask my question one more time, but look directly at the fox. "Have I ever told you that I love you?"

The fox stands on its back two legs for just a second, and then falls forward again on all four, scampers quickly over to my hand, and butts her head against it. When it turns its eyes to me, it stares for just a few seconds and then turns and flees into the woods.

I stand quickly and turn in the direction the fox ran, and swear, for just a second, in the shadows, that I see Sydney. I blink, though, and the image is gone. In that instance, so is the deep pain that surrounded my heart for almost a month. I shake my head and then look at her grave, bend down, and place a kiss on my hand and then press it into dirt. "I do, so, so much."

And then I turn and head back down the hill to the only other girl that will ever hold my heart.

The End

ACKNOWLEDGMENTS

There are always so many people you want to thank after you finish writing a book, and for those of you who already know me, I tend to get wordy… For once, I'm going to try and keep this relatively short. Wish me luck…

First and foremost, a huge thank you to my son, and my very own rock star, Tyler. Sydney's poems are actually Tyler's songs. Songs he'd already written and that I loved, so I wrote scenes in the book that enabled me to use them; his words. If you want to hear his music, you can find him on Spotify at Tyler Legare. The songs in this book, Choices, Friday's, and In Your Arms (Alaska), are being released on 4/28/2018, on an album titled Alaska. Check him out; he's amazing. Tyler, you slay me with your talent, your drive, and your passion. I love you.

Thank you to my rock, the better half of me, the person who can always make me laugh, and still loves me like crazy, my husband Doug. You built me a palace of an office, you put up my bookcases, you share my every post and support my every dream. I love you so much and thank the heavens every day that you asked me to dance all those years ago. Tommy, thanks for every supportive hug, bringing me coffee, giving me more hugs, telling me I'm an amazing mom, and oh yeah, did I mention the amazing hugs? Felicia, thanks for styling out my swag, having the patience of a saint while you do, and for being everything I could want in a daughter.

I wouldn't be half the author I am without the support of the amazing Indie community I'm a part of. Helene Cuji, thank you for your constant support, friendship and love, but especially for introducing me to my book bestie, Haylee Thorne. I think every writer needs a ying to their yang to help find their balance, and I have definitely found that in her. Okay, perhaps the balance thing is still an issue, but I blame the champagne, which again, is Haylee's fault. Haylee, thanks for every phone call where you made me laugh, told me to snap out of it, reminded me I was good enough, helped me through a chapter, or just to talk about our day. I cannot wait to see what's to come for us! Love your face.

Thanks to Amanda Walker for this amazingly gorgeous cover, and for all your support and friendship. I can send you a message with a vision in my head, and you deliver every time. I'd just be a blank canvas without you my friend, and oh how boring that would be!

Cindi Medley, Cindy Wolken, Julie Smith and Haylee, thank you for being the first to read this story, share your thoughts, and then threaten to kill me as ugly crying commenced. Cindy, an extra thank you for staying up half the night to help me piece together the perfect ending for the book; it was a struggle! Cindi, thanks for my crown(s). It's fucking awesome being the queen of my castle!! I truly appreciate every bit of feedback and support you all give me and am so humbled by your friendships!

Thanks to my editor Kendra, who by the way also threatened to kill me, but also makes this book ultimately what it is, and that's perfect. You've been so instrumental in helping me to grow as a writer and a story teller and I thank you from the bottom of my heart.

I hate listing names, because I always know I'm going to miss someone, but off the top of my head, Andrea Bills, April Moran, Lauren Valderrama, Dusty Summerford, Gina Moody, Carolina Mamos, Nikki Pearce, Christina Butrum, Taryn Steele, Janine Bosco, Cat Wright, Letha Hanover, and CE Johnson: thank you really doesn't say enough for all your shares, your comments, your support, but I hope you know how very much it means to me. Things have been rough in our book world as of late, and having a circle of friends like you around is not only comforting, it's a privilege.

And to my readers on my group page, Michelle's Box of Jewels, thank you, thank you, thank you for all your support, all our fun live feeds, your friendships, and all the laughter you bring me. Having you behind me, holding me up, cheering me on, makes my world such a better place!

Love Notes Play List

Just Breathe by Pearl Jam
Crazy by Patsy Cline
Linger by The Cranberries
Look Good in my Shirt Keith Urban
Ring of Fire by Johnny Cash
The Gambler by Kenny Rogers
In Your Arms by Tyler Legare
Choices by Tyler Legare
Perfect by Ed Sheeran
Friday's by Tyler Legare
Here Without You by Three Doors Down

You can find this playlist on Spotify, under Love Notes, The Book
Please note: Songs by Tyler Legare won't be available until 4/28/18

ABOUT THE AUTHOR

Michelle Windsor is a wife, mom, and a writer who lives North of Boston with her family. When she isn't writing, she's been known to partake in good wine and good food with her family and friends. She's a voracious reader, loves to hike with her German shepherd, Roman, enjoys a good romance movie and may be slightly obsessed with Outlander.

www.authormichellewindsor.com

facebook.com/authormwindsor
instagram.com/author_michelle_windsor

ALSO BY MICHELLE WINDSOR

The Auction Series
The Winning Bid
The Final Bid

Losing Hope
Breaking Benjamin (Releasing May 2018)

Made in the USA
Columbia, SC
05 January 2025